The Self Speaks

A Dialogue With Infinity

Adamus Ananda

DEDICATION

To my parents, Marianna and Stanisław,
with deep gratitude for their loving care and guidance and for
raising me with strength and compassion.

To my spiritual guides and mentors – the Mighty I AM
Presence, Jesus Christ, St. Germain, Patanjali, Anandamayi
Ma, Sai Baba, Buddha, Lady Nada, Ashtavakra, Dattatreya,
Diamond Mother of Dragons, Beautiful Lady, Fire Dragon,
Christ Consciousness Beings, Eckhart Tolle, Mooji, Ancestors,
Ascended Masters, and all Beings…
Thank you for the wisdom, light, and love that have inspired
me on this path. Your presence has been my guiding star.

And to you, dear reader,
may this book be a source of inspiration and a gentle reminder
that the true Self is always within you, waiting to be
discovered. May each word bring you closer to the peace and
joy that are your essence.

Finally, to myself,
for the courage to embark on this journey and trust in the
unfolding of the Self.

Table of Contents

Introduction_____1

   *Why Did I Write This Book?*_____1

   *Who is the Reader?*_____2

   *How to Use This Book*_____4

Chapter 1: Who Am I?_____7

   *The Self Without a Body*_____7

   *Timeless and Spaceless*_____9

   *The Self Knows No Fear*_____12

Chapter 2: What the Self Is Not_____16

   *The Illusion of the Body*_____16

   *Thoughts and Emotions: Moments That Come and Go*_____20

   *I Am Not the Experiencer*_____24

Chapter 3: The Mind as the Director of Experience_____30

   *The Mechanisms of the Mind*_____31

   *How Does the Mind Create Dramas and Conflicts?*_____34

   *Transcending the Limitations of the Mind*_____39

Chapter 4: Playing with Illusion_____43

   *The Game of Life: Observation and Purpose*_____43

   *The World as a Dreaming Illusion: Understanding and
Liberation*_____48

   *Playing in Silence: Peace in Chaos*_____53

Chapter 5: The Self as Freedom_____58

   *Let Go of the Chains You Never Had*_____58

   *Effortless Freedom*_____63

   *Independence from Fate*_____68

Chapter 6: The Joy of the Self_____74

   *Laughing at the Illusion*_____74

True Happiness _____79

Living in the World, but Beyond It _____84

Chapter 7: Who I Have Always Been _____90

I Am Infinity _____90

The Oneness of Everything _____94

The End of the Game _____100

Chapter 8: The Stillness and Silence of the Self _____106

Stillness in the Heart of the Storm _____105

How Silence is the Source of Everything _____110

The World as Movement, the Self as Stillness _____115

Chapter 9: The Self Beyond Time and Space _____121

Time: Just Another Illusion _____121

Space as a Game of Perception _____126

Eternity in Every Moment _____131

Chapter 10: Transcending Duality _____137

Good and Evil: Two Sides of the Same Coin _____137

The Unity of Opposites _____142

Ultimate Freedom: Beyond Desire and Fear _____147

Chapter 11: Discovering the Self: Practical Guidance _____154

Do not search for the Self outside; realise it has always been within you. _____154

Daily Practices of Presence _____157

Meditation and Contemplation of the Self _____167

How to Cultivate Awareness of the Self in Every Moment ____170

Conclusion _____175

Laughter in Peace _____175

Appendix: Frequently Asked Questions About the Self _____180

Q&A with the Self (With a Lighthearted Twist) _____180

Introduction

Why Did I Write This Book?

I have often asked myself a question that perhaps you have also pondered: Who am I, really? In a world filled with constant noise, struggles, and rush, many of us are searching for the answer to this fundamental question. My search led me to a profound understanding that the answer does not lie in external circumstances or in what the mind tells us. The answer has always been, and will always be, within – the Self, which is the source of everything.

I wrote this book to help you and myself look beyond the illusions that the world feeds us and to discover the truth that is not subject to change, the passage of time, or space. I wanted to create a guide that wouldn't overwhelm with difficult philosophies or impose specific beliefs. Instead, I wanted the Self – your true, eternal Self – to speak directly to you without intermediaries or complicated theories, simply with humor and clarity.

Why is this book important? Because it reminds us of something we all already know but often forget: that we are more than the body, the mind, or emotions. We are the boundless Self, a presence of infinite awareness, silently witnessing the world from a space of stillness and peace. My hope is that everyone who picks up this book will not just read about this truth, but *remember* it—as something deeply familiar, a core part of who we've always been.

Perhaps you are asking questions that no one has been able to answer. The questions that provoke you to dig deeper into your own existence. Perhaps you are experiencing moments of doubt, fear, or confusion. Or maybe you just feel that there must be something more. Whatever has brought you here, this book is an invitation to return home – to discover what has always been, is, and will be: the true You.

Who is the Reader?

You. Who you truly are goes beyond your name, profession, life story, and even what you think of yourself at this moment.

If you've come across this book, it's likely that you are searching for something more. Perhaps you are asking yourself questions about the meaning of existence, about who you really are, or why life is often filled with tension, uncertainty, and suffering. Maybe you feel that the answers the world has offered so far have been insufficient.

It doesn't matter whether you are at the beginning of your spiritual journey or have been exploring these topics for years. **This book is for anyone seeking to know themselves on a deeper, more meaningful level.** Maybe you're thriving in your professional life, reaching goals and milestones, but still feel an emptiness inside—an inner void that no amount of material success seems to fill. Or maybe you've reached a point where you've had enough of the constant chase for something that always seems just out of reach—peace, happiness, fulfillment.

As a reader of this book, you may be facing questions about the essence of life and death, good and evil, and what it truly means to be free. Or perhaps you simply long to experience the peace that seems so elusive. Regardless of where you come from, what you do, or what your experiences have been, one thing connects us all: the desire to discover who we really are. We all want to find that place within ourselves where there is no fear, no uncertainty, no pain.

The Self, which speaks in this book, addresses you directly. Not the role you play in the world, not your profession, achievements, or titles. It speaks to you as an eternal being who has always existed, who is here now, and who will always be. This book is a journey that you are embarking on—not as a body, not as a mind, but as pure, infinite awareness.

So, who is the reader? The reader is someone ready to go beyond the surface of life's external forms and uncover what is real, what is timeless. They seek to touch eternity, to look beyond the fleeting and connect with their true, unchanging nature.

How to Use This Book

This book is not your typical spiritual guide. You won't find complex philosophical theories or rigid dogmas to follow here. The Self: A Dialogue with Infinity is a conversation—a conversation between you and your deepest, truest Self. Every chapter, every word, is an invitation to reflect, to ponder who you truly are.

You don't need to rush through this book, reading it from cover to cover in one sitting. On the contrary, I encourage you to pause after each chapter or even after each paragraph and take time to truly contemplate what you've read. The questions that arise in your mind are a natural part of this journey. Instead of seeking immediate answers, allow yourself the time to let these questions mature within you. The answers you seek won't come from the outside—you will find them within.

Each of us is at a different stage in our spiritual journey, so this book doesn't require any specific knowledge or experience. You can return to these chapters time and again, each visit revealing new layers and insights. Some parts may stir deep emotions within you, while others might feel challenging to fully understand—and that's perfectly okay. Let the text work through you gradually, dissolving old beliefs and opening doors to deeper understanding.

I recommend reading this book in a quiet, peaceful place where you can focus on its content without distractions. You might also consider keeping a journal to record your reflections, insights, and the questions that arise. This will help you track your journey and, over time, notice how your perception of yourself and the world changes.

This book doesn't provide you with ready-made answers, because the answers you seek are already within you.

The Self Speaks: A Dialogue with Infinity serves as a mirror, allowing you to see your true Self—not through the lens of illusion, but with the clarity of awareness. Use it as a tool to discover what has always been and will always be—your eternal, unchanging Self.

I invite you to approach this book with an open heart and mind, allowing each word to guide you deeper into the discovery of who you are. This is not a book to simply read. It's a book to meditate on, to reflect upon, and to live with.

Welcome to the dialogue with infinity.

Chapter 1: Who Am I?

The Self Without a Body

When you look in the mirror, what do you see? A face, a body, perhaps some imperfections you wish weren't there, or features you admire. But let your true self ask you—*is that really you?* Is that reflection in the mirror truly the essence of who you are, or is there something more meaningful to it, something beyond the image staring back at you?

The answer is simple: no. What you see in the mirror is just the outer shell, the physical form that carries you through life. But you, the true you, are much more than that. You are not the body that grows, changes, ages, and eventually fades away. You are the awareness behind all of it—the one who witnesses these changes but is never touched by them.

Think about it: you were there when your body was a child. As it grew into adolescence, you were there. Now, as it continues to age, you are still there. The body may change, but you do not. What does that tell you? It tells you that you are not the body. You are the constant presence that observes the body, the unchanging witness to all its transformations.

When you say, "I am tired," or "I am hungry," you're not really talking about you. You're talking about the body. But your body is not you—it's something you experience, like a piece of clothing you wear. Just as you would change your clothes at the end of the day, the body is something temporary, while you are eternal.

So, if you are not the body, what are you? You are pure consciousness. You are the awareness that observes everything, without judgment, without attachment. You are the silent witness to life's ups and downs, yet they never affect you. When the body feels pain, you are not in pain—you simply observe the sensation. When the body feels pleasure, you are not the one experiencing it—you observe that too.

Imagine standing in front of a mirror, seeing your reflection, but knowing deep inside that the reflection is not the real you. It's just an image. The same applies to your body and the world around you. These are just reflections of the Self, fleeting images that pass before the true you, which remains untouched and unchanged.

To realise this is to take a significant step toward understanding the truth of who you are. You are not what you see in the mirror. You are not the body that moves through the world. You are the consciousness that sees, that knows, that is. The body may come and go, but you, the Self, remain forever.

So the next time you look in the mirror, smile at the body but remember: I am not that.

Timeless and Spaceless

Now that you understand you are not the body, we can go deeper. Let's talk about time and space—the things that seem to define our entire existence. We wake up at certain times, we live in certain places, and everything around us is measured in hours, days, and distances. But here's the secret: You, the Self, exist beyond all of this. You are timeless and spaceless.

Let's begin by exploring time. From the moment you were born, you were taught that time is linear, moving in one direction: past, present, future. But does that concept truly apply to you—the Self? Think about a moment of joy or sadness in your life—doesn't it still exist vividly in your memory, as if it were happening right now? Time didn't erase that experience. In truth, time is just another concept, an illusion that passes through your awareness, while *you* remain timeless, untouched by its flow.

The Self doesn't experience time because it is beyond time. Time is like a river, constantly flowing, while you are the shore, eternally still, watching the water pass by. The Self doesn't age. It doesn't have a "before" or "after." It just is. While the body grows older, the Self remains untouched by the passage of time. You were here before this body, and you will remain long after it is gone.

Now, let's turn to space. We often say things like, "I am here, and you are there." We measure distances, and we navigate through space, but that is all from the perspective of the body and mind. The Self, however, is beyond such limitations. Where are you, really? Are you confined to your physical location, the spot where your body is sitting or standing right now? No. You are everywhere and nowhere at the same time.

The Self is not located in space—it contains space. Space exists within your awareness, just as time does. In deep moments of meditation, haven't you felt a sense of vastness, like you are expanding beyond your body, beyond the room you're in as if the boundaries of space dissolve? That's because the Self is boundless. It is the vastness itself, and no physical distance can confine it.

Think of space as a stage where the play of life happens. The actors, the props, the scenery—they all change. But the stage remains unchanged, no matter what's placed upon it. You, the Self, are a depiction of that stage. All of life's events—places, people, and circumstances—play out on you, but none of it defines you. You remain as spacious as ever, untouched by what moves across you.

To put it simply: you are neither "here" nor "there." You are everywhere, always. The body moves through time and space, but the Self is the timeless, spaceless awareness in which both time and space arise.

So, who are you, really? You are that which has no beginning and no end, that which exists outside of the limits of time and space. You are the eternal presence, the infinite awareness in which everything unfolds, but which remains unchanged. Time may flow, and space may expand or contract, but you? You are beyond it all.

The Self Knows No Fear

Fear. It's something we all know intimately, isn't it? The fear of loss, the fear of pain, the fear of the unknown. It creeps into our minds, sometimes like a whisper, other times like a roar. But here's the truth: The Self knows no fear. How could it? Fear is born from attachment to the unreal, and the Self is rooted in what is truly real.

Let's explore this a little more deeply. What exactly is fear? At its core, fear is a reaction to something we perceive as a threat. But a threat to what? To the body, to the mind, to our possessions, to our identity. Fear is always tied to the temporary, the changeable, the fragile—things that come and go. But you, the Self, are none of those things. You are eternal, unchanging, and invulnerable. How can you fear losing something when nothing can touch your true nature?

Imagine this: You're watching a movie, and in the film, the characters are in danger. The music swells, the tension builds, and your heart starts to race. For a moment, you forget that it's just a movie, and you feel the fear as if it were real. But then, a moment of clarity hits you: none of it is real. It's just light on a screen, an illusion created to evoke emotion. The fear tends to fade away because you remember that you're safe, untouched by the events playing out in front of you. Just like a movie can't truly have a life-changing impact on you, the things you experience are also separate from your inner, unchanging self.

In the same way, fear in life arises from our attachment to the illusion—the belief that we are the body, that we are the mind, that we are the identities we've built. We fear losing these things because we've mistaken them for who we are. But once you realise that these are all just part of the grand illusion, like the movie on the screen, the fear dissolves. How can you be afraid of losing what was never truly real to begin with?

Consider the fear of death, one of the most powerful fears we face. We fear the end of the body, the end of our identity. But if you are not the body, and you are not the mind, what is there to fear? Death is simply the ending of the illusion, the fading of the temporary. The Self remains untouched and eternal, just as it always has been. The end of a dream does not affect the dreamer. You are the dreamer, not the dream.

Another common fear is the fear of failure—of not being good enough, of losing what we've worked for. But failure, too, is tied to the illusion. It's tied to the idea that we are what we achieve, what we own, or how others see us. But the Self is beyond all achievements, beyond all perceptions. It is whole and complete in itself. How can you fear failure when you are already perfect beyond the need for validation or success?

Fear is like a shadow. It looks real, it feels real, but it has no substance of its own. It can only exist in the presence of light—specifically, the light of your awareness, which mistakenly shines on the illusion. When you shift your awareness back to the Self, the fear fades because it was never real to begin with.

The Self is unshakable, immovable, and beyond harm. It cannot be threatened, it cannot be diminished, and it cannot be lost. So, fear—whether it's of death, loss, failure, or the unknown—is just an echo of illusion. When you see the world for what it truly is—an ever-changing projection on the screen of consciousness—you come to realise there is nothing to fear. The constant change around you doesn't touch the core of who you are!

In the world of illusion, fear has a grip on those who believe they are fragile, temporary beings. But you, the Self, are neither fragile nor temporary. You are eternal, invincible, and unafraid. Fear only exists when you forget who you truly are. When you remember, fear has no place to stand.

So, take a deep breath. Relax. Let go of the fear that clings to the unreal. You are the Self, the fearless witness to it all. Nothing in this world of illusion can touch you. Nothing can make you afraid because you are beyond all that is fleeting. Fear is an illusion, and you are the truth.

Chapter 2: What the Self Is Not

The Illusion of the Body

Let's start by addressing one of the most deeply ingrained illusions we carry: the belief that we are the body. From the moment we are born, the body becomes our central reference point. We identify with it, we dress it, we care for it, and we even define ourselves by how it looks, how it feels, and how it functions. But here's a fundamental truth: The body is not who you are. It's just like a piece of clothing, something you wear for a time, but not something that defines the essence of who you truly are.

Think of the body as a set of clothes you put on for this lifetime. Just as you change clothes when they wear out, so too do you change bodies when the time comes. The body you had as a child is not the same as the one you have now. It's grown, aged, and transformed. But despite all these changes, you, the Self, have remained exactly the same. The body is temporary and constantly in flux, but the Self is eternal and unchanging. Just as you remain the same person regardless of whether

16

you're wearing jeans, a suit, or pajamas, you remain the same regardless of what form your body takes.

Let's go deeper. What happens when you're asleep? The body rests, the senses shut down, and yet, you continue to exist. In deep sleep, you are not conscious of the body, and yet the Self remains. This shows us that even when the body is inactive, the essence of who you are doesn't depend on it. The body can be still, unconscious, or even absent, and you, the awareness behind it, remain untouched. This is a key indication that the body is not the true "essence"—it is simply a vehicle you are temporarily inhabiting.

Now, think about how much effort we put into maintaining the body. We feed it, exercise it, dress it, and sometimes even obsess over its appearance. But all this effort is being poured into something that is, by its very nature, temporary and fleeting. The body ages, gets sick, and eventually passes away. Yet, throughout all of this, the Self remains constant, untouched by time, disease, or decay. Just as you wouldn't define yourself by the clothes you wear, you shouldn't define yourself by the body you temporarily inhabit.

Another way to look at it is through the lens of change.

Everything about the body changes—its size, shape, strength, and even its ability to function. You may feel strong one day and weak the next. You may look youthful now, and in time, age will leave its marks. But ask yourself this: If everything about the body can change, then how can it be who you truly are? The real "core" of your being must be something that doesn't change, something that remains constant no matter what. That constant, unchanging presence is the Self. The body is simply a reflection of the ever-changing world around you, while the Self is the eternal witness to those changes.

Let's take it even further. Imagine that your body undergoes some drastic transformation. Does that change who you are at your core? Of course not. You may feel the loss or the change in the body, but you, the awareness behind it, are not diminished in any way. The Self is whole and complete, regardless of the state of the body. Just as cutting a piece off your clothing doesn't change who you are, losing or changing part of the body doesn't affect your true essence.

The body is also tied to identity. We often say things like "I am tall," "I am short," "I am strong," or "I am weak," as if these physical traits define us. But if you were to strip away all those labels, what would remain? You would still exist, still be aware, still be conscious. The body is just a temporary form, a tool for experiencing the physical world. It's not who you are, but rather something you use to navigate the realm of the senses.

When you don a new outfit, you might admire how it looks or feels, but deep down, you know that you are not the embodiment of the garments you wear. In the same way, you can admire or care for the body, but deep down, you must remember that you are not the body. You are the observer. You are the one who experiences life through the body, but you are not defined by it. Just as clothing fades and is replaced, the body will come and go, while the Self remains constant, timeless, and free.

So, the next time you find yourself identifying with the body, remember this: I am not this body. Just as clothes do not define who you are, the body does not define the Self. The body is a tool, a vessel, a temporary form, but it is not the essence of your being. You are the consciousness, the awareness that transcends the physical. You are eternal, unchanging, and free, while the body is just a fleeting garment you wear for this journey through life.

Understanding this is the first step toward freeing yourself from the limitations of the physical world. The body may age, suffer, or change, but you are untouched by any of it. You are the Self—timeless, spaceless, and unbound by the illusions of the physical form.

Thoughts and Emotions: Moments That Come and Go

If the body doesn't define who you are, what about your thoughts and emotions? These seem even closer to you, don't they? After all, you feel them so deeply and experience them so personally. Your thoughts often feel like an intimate expression of yourself, and your emotions can seem like the very core of your being. But here's the truth: You are not your thoughts or emotions. Like clouds drifting across the sky, thoughts and emotions are temporary, ever-changing, and ultimately separate from who you truly are.

Let's begin with thoughts. They come in waves, seemingly out of nowhere. Sometimes, they're calm and peaceful; other times, they're turbulent and chaotic. You may have noticed that your mind can't seem to stay still for long. One moment you're thinking about what you need to do tomorrow, and the next, you're remembering something from years ago. The mind is constantly in motion, like a stream flowing endlessly. But here's the key: you are not the stream. You are the one observing the stream.

Thoughts are like visitors in your home. They come, they stay for a while, and then they leave. But you, the Self, are like the home itself—stable, unchanging, and unaffected by the comings and goings of these mental visitors. Just because a thought appears in your mind doesn't mean it defines you. In fact, have you ever noticed how quickly your thoughts can change? One moment you're certain of something, and the next, you're questioning it. If thoughts were truly "you," they wouldn't change so easily.

The same applies to emotions. Emotions are powerful forces that rise within you, often without warning. They can feel overwhelming—like waves crashing on the shore, sometimes gentle, sometimes fierce. But emotions, like thoughts, are temporary. No matter how intense an emotion feels in the moment, it eventually passes. Think back to a time when you were extremely happy or deeply sad. At the time, it might have felt like that emotion would last forever, but it didn't. It faded, just like all emotions do.

Emotions are like weather patterns. One day the sun is shining, the next it's stormy, but the sky itself remains unchanged. You, the Self, are like the sky. Emotions pass through you, but they do not alter your true nature. They are simply fleeting experiences, while you remain the constant, unchanging awareness behind them. When you feel happiness, you are the one who is aware of that happiness. When you feel sadness, you are the one who observes the sadness. But in both cases, you are the observer, not the emotion itself.

Let's take a step back and consider how we often talk about emotions. We say things like "I am angry" or "I am sad," as if those emotions define who we are in that moment. But that's not true. You are not angry—you are the one experiencing anger. You are not sad—you are the one observing the sadness. The emotion is just a temporary state, but you, the Self, remain unchanged by it. Imagine yourself as the stillness beneath the surface of the ocean. The waves of emotion rise and fall, but the deep waters remain calm and undisturbed. That is the essence of the Self.

There's another important thing to realise about thoughts and emotions: they are often reactive. They arise in response to the world around you—what people say, what happens during the day, or even memories of the past. But the Self is not reactive.

The Self is pure awareness, untouched by the external world. Thoughts and emotions belong to the mind, which is constantly reacting to stimuli, but the Self simply observes, silently and peacefully, without being pulled in by these reactions.

Let's consider thoughts again. Have you ever tried to stop thinking, to quiet your mind completely? It's not easy. The mind is always generating new thoughts, one after another. But here's something fascinating: even while all those thoughts are flowing, there's a part of you that can observe them. You can sit quietly and watch your thoughts pass by, like watching cars drive down a road. If you can observe your thoughts, then you must be separate from them. They are not you. They are simply passing phenomena, while you remain the still observer.

The same applies to emotions. Even in the middle of a strong emotion—whether it's joy, anger, or sadness—there's a part of you that can step back and simply observe what you're feeling. That part of you, the observer, is the Self. The Self doesn't get caught up in the emotional storm. It watches from a place of stillness and peace, knowing that, like all things, this too shall pass.

In everyday life, we often let our thoughts and emotions define us. We think, "I am this thought," or "I am this feeling." But that's an illusion. Thoughts and emotions are just passing experiences, temporary movements of the mind. They are not the essence of who you are. The Self is beyond thoughts and emotions, beyond the mind's constant chatter. It is the silent witness to all of these experiences, but it is never touched or defined by them.

So, the next time you find yourself lost in a whirlwind of thoughts or emotions, remember this: I am not my thoughts. I am not my emotions. They are just moments that come and go, like clouds passing through the sky. But I, the Self, am the unchanging awareness, the eternal witness. Thoughts and emotions are fleeting, but I am forever.

I Am Not the Experiencer

Now that we've uncovered the truth that you are not the body, nor the thoughts or emotions that pass through the mind, let's dive even deeper. There's another illusion to dissolve—the idea that you are the one experiencing everything that happens in life. The belief that you are the doer, the experiencer, is at the very heart of the illusion, and it's one of the most deeply rooted. But here's the reality: You are not the experiencer. You are the witness—the silent observer of everything that unfolds. Life is like a movie, and you are the one watching it, untouched and uninvolved.

Let's use the metaphor of a movie to make this clear. Imagine sitting in a movie theater. The lights dim, the screen flickers to life, and the story begins to unfold. There are characters with their own emotions, conflicts, triumphs, and failures. You might get caught up in the plot—laughing, crying, or gasping at the twists and turns. But no matter how engrossed you become, deep down you know it's not real. You know that you are not one of the characters. You're simply watching it all happen from the comfort of your seat.

This is exactly how the Self experiences life. The world, with all its dramas, emotions, and experiences, is like that movie on the screen. It feels real, it pulls you in, but at its core, it's an illusion—a grand play. And you, the Self, are the one sitting in the audience, watching it all unfold. You are the witness, the observer, not one of the actors in the story. The events of life— pleasure, pain, joy, sorrow—are like scenes in the movie. They come and go, but you, the Self, remain unaffected, untouched by it all.

Think about how often you say things like, "I am experiencing this" or "I am going through that." This language reinforces the idea that you are personally involved in every aspect of life, that you are the one living it. But this is a misunderstanding. The Self is not involved. It is the pure awareness behind all experiences, but it does not participate in them. The Self doesn't feel joy or pain, it doesn't struggle or succeed. It simply watches as these experiences pass by, like scenes in the movie.

Imagine watching a storm through a window. The wind howls, the rain pours down, and the sky darkens with clouds. But inside, you are safe and dry. You're not in the storm—you're just observing it from a distance. Life's experiences are like that storm. They rage and swirl outside, but you, the Self, are sitting safely behind the window, unaffected. The Self is the observer, not the one caught up in the chaos.

Here's where it gets tricky. The mind is very good at convincing you that you are deeply involved in life, that you are the one who is doing everything, feeling everything, and controlling everything. But the truth is, the mind is just another part of the movie. It's another character playing its role. The Self, however, is beyond the mind. It is the space in which the mind operates, the silent background against which thoughts, emotions, and experiences appear and disappear. This is why, even in the most intense moments of life—whether it's a moment of great joy or deep sorrow—there's always a part of you that remains untouched, a part that simply observes. That part is the Self. It doesn't get involved in the drama. It doesn't try to control or change the outcome. It just watches, with perfect clarity and detachment.

To understand this fully, let's return to the metaphor of the movie. When you watch a film, you might feel connected to the characters, but you never truly forget that it's all just a story. The emotions you feel are part of the experience, but you know they're not real. When the movie ends, you stand up, walk out of the theater, and return to your real life, completely unaffected by what you just watched. The same is true for the Self. Life's experiences are just a temporary movie. They play out on the screen of consciousness, but they don't define or change who you are. When the movie of life ends, the Self remains, untouched and eternal.

What's the key difference between the Self and the experiencer? The experiencer believes it is part of the story. It believes it's the one feeling the emotions, making the decisions, and living the life. The Self, on the other hand, knows that it is simply observing the story. It is not involved in any of it. The experiencer gets caught up in the illusion, while the Self remains free from it.

Let's also consider how this applies to everyday life. When something good happens, you might say, "I am happy." When something bad happens, you might say, "I am sad." But in both cases, it's not truly you who is happy or sad. These are just experiences passing through the mind, like waves on the surface of the ocean. The Self is the deep, still water beneath the waves, completely unaffected by the highs and lows on the surface.

When you fully realise that you are not the experiencer, life becomes much simpler. You no longer feel the need to cling to the good moments or resist the bad ones. You understand that all experiences are just part of the movie, and you, the Self, are the one watching it all with calm detachment. You are free from the push and pull of life's ups and downs because you know that none of it truly touches you.

So, who are you really? You are not the experiencer. You are the witness, the silent observer of life's movie. The events of life may come and go, but you remain untouched, just as the screen remains unchanged no matter what film is projected onto it. Life is the movie, and you, the Self, are the eternal witness, sitting peacefully in the audience, watching the story unfold without being drawn into it.

Chapter 3: The Mind as the Director of Experience

The mind plays a crucial role in our lives. It designs, interprets, and creates the scenarios that fill our daily experiences. It is like a director, controlling how we perceive reality and how we respond to external stimuli. However, as mentioned earlier, the mind is not the screen on which this movie of life is projected —it is merely a tool that helps create what we see. Understanding this subtle difference is key to discovering our true nature.

The mind operates at the level of interpretation, creating meanings and assigning structures to reality. When you look at the world, it is not reality itself that affects your experience, but rather how your mind interprets these events. The mind gives meaning to every event, creating the storyline you believe to be reality. However, the mind, as a director, operates with limited resources. It focuses on the past and future, rarely allowing you to be fully present in the here and now.

Many people identify with the mind, forgetting that the mind is just a tool. What appears on the screen of your life is not entirely controlled by the mind. The true screen, on which everything unfolds, is the Self—your true, unchanging nature. In this chapter, you will learn how the mind, as a perfect director, guides your life, creating the illusion of separateness, while the true essence remains unaffected by what the mind projects.

The Mechanisms of the Mind

To understand how the mind acts as a director, we must first examine its mechanisms. The mind operates on several levels, each influencing your experience of the world. We can distinguish the main mechanisms of the mind's operation as follows:

Thoughts as the primary tool of creation

The mind generates thoughts, which shape our perception of reality. Every thought affects how we perceive the external world and the emotions we feel. When the mind produces negative thoughts, our experience of the world is filled with fear, sadness, or anger. On the other hand, positive thoughts can evoke joy and peace. However, the key lesson of this chapter is that thoughts are merely a product of the mind—they are not reality. They create an image of the world, but they are not the world itself.

The construction of identity

The mind constructs identity, basing it on past experiences, beliefs, and expectations for the future. It creates the story of "the core of your being," with which we identify, leading us to believe that we are our thoughts, beliefs, and emotions. However, this identity is merely a creation of the mind—an illusion of separateness. In reality, the Self, which is our true nature, remains untouched by these stories the mind continually constructs and reinforces.

Projection of the future and past

The mind tends to escape the present, directing our attention to the past or future. Through analyzing what has happened and planning what is to come, the mind keeps us in a state of constant worry and thinking about what could have been or what should have happened. Instead of being in the present moment, we are trapped in a continuous chase of thoughts. Only in the present can you connect with the Self, which is always beyond the limitations of time and space.

Perceptual Filter

The mind acts like a filter, processing information through its beliefs, judgments, and past experiences. This means that every moment you experience is interpreted by the mind based on previous experiences. This mechanism influences how you perceive the world and how you react to events. The mind works like a lens through which you see reality, but it never shows you the complete picture. Its interpretations are limited to what it knows and has learned.

The Illusion of Control

The mind tends to believe that it can control everything in our lives. It tries to predict, plan, and control future events, which leads to stress and anxiety. However, the control that the mind seeks to maintain is illusory. Reality often slips out of attempts to control it, and true freedom comes when we realise that controlling everything is not possible. The mind creates the illusion that we can influence every aspect of our lives, while the true Self remains aware that everything is part of a larger order that cannot be fully controlled.

Emotions as a Product of Thoughts

The mind generates emotions based on the thoughts it creates. When a negative thought arises, it is often accompanied by a negative emotion, such as fear, anger, or sadness. Conversely, positive thoughts lead to pleasant emotions, like joy or peace. Emotions are, therefore, a reaction to thoughts, not to reality itself. Understanding this mechanism allows you to gain distance from emotions and stop identifying with them.

These mechanisms of the mind are key to understanding how our perception of reality operates. In the next part of this chapter, we will explore how we can discover the Self, which is beyond the mind, and how to disengage from its game to experience life fully from the level of conscious presence.

How Does the Mind Create Dramas and Conflicts?

The mind has an incredible ability to create complex dramas and conflicts that seem entirely real. These dramas are an inherent part of the game the mind plays—a game based on interpretations, judgments, beliefs, and emotions. Each of us experiences these dramas daily, yet we rarely realise that it is not reality but the mind that is their main creator.

At the outset, it's important to understand that the mind has a tendency to complicate reality. It is like a screenwriter who continuously writes new scenarios. In truth, most situations are simple, but the mind adds layers of interpretation, turning them into more complicated stories that often lead to conflicts. It is in these interpretations where the source of the dramas lies.

The mind operates on the following primary mechanisms that contribute most significantly to the creation of dramas and conflicts:

Judgments and Categorization

The mind constantly judges and categorizes. It divides the world into what is "good" and "bad," "right" and "wrong," "beneficial" and "harmful." In every moment, the mind creates narratives based on these judgments and classifications. These evaluations often lead to internal conflicts and external disputes because every decision or event is analyzed in terms of its "good" and "bad" consequences. For example, when someone insults you, the mind immediately forms a judgment: "I have been hurt," followed by: "I need to defend myself" or "I need to react." These judgments trigger emotions and, as a result, lead to conflict.

The Illusion of Separateness

The mind creates dramas because it perceives the world through the lens of separateness. It sees us as separate individuals operating in a separate, hostile world where we must fight for our place. This perception leads to conflicts with others because it assumes that we are divided and must protect our own interests. In reality, dramas often arise from the fear that others might take something from us, harm us, or stand in our way of achieving what we desire.

Dramas in the mind often stem from fear—fear of loss, failure, fear of the unknown. These fears create the belief that we need to control, predict, or change something to avoid pain. Every drama begins with a thought that says: "Something is wrong," or "I need to do something about this." The mind creates scenarios full of conflicts and emotions based on the illusion that reality is a threat, and we must react, fight, or avoid it.

Role Creation and Expectations

The mind creates dramas when it starts assigning specific roles and expectations to ourselves and others. For example, in everyday life, we play various roles—partner, friend, employee —and each of these roles comes with certain expectations. When these expectations are not met, the mind immediately creates conflict because it believes reality should be different. In this way, the mind creates drama around what others should or should not do, how they should treat us, and what outcomes should result from our actions.

Exaggerated Emotional Reactions

Dramas and conflicts are largely the result of exaggerated emotional reactions, which the mind amplifies. For example, a small situation can quickly escalate into a big drama when the mind starts attaching significant meaning to it. If someone doesn't respond to our message, the mind may create an entire narrative about what that means—that the person is ignoring us, doesn't respect us, or that something is wrong with our relationship. From a simple event with little significance, the mind creates a complex drama.

Projection into the Future

The mind often creates dramas by attempting to predict the future and worrying about what will happen. It constructs scenarios that have never occurred and likely never will, but the mere act of imagining them causes anxiety and conflict. It is the mind, painting worst-case scenarios, that generates dramas that provoke fear and stress.

All of these mechanisms of the mind lead to dramas that seem real but are, in fact, merely projections, illusions created by the mind. When we understand that the mind is the creator of these dramas, we begin to notice the distance between ourselves and the stories it tells us. As a result, we can stop engaging in dramas and conflicts that are not real but simply illusions generated by the mind.

In the following sections of this chapter, we will analyze how the mind uses these mechanisms to keep us in a state of illusion and how we can break free from this cycle of drama to discover the true nature of the Self, which exists beyond these mechanisms.

Transcending the Limitations of the Mind

The mind is an incredibly powerful tool, but at the same time, it is limiting. As we've already noted, the mind tends to create dramas, generate conflicts, and trap us in a world of the illusion of separateness. However, in order to experience the true Self, we must learn to transcend these limitations and see that the mind is not our ultimate identity. Although powerful, the mind cannot touch the truth that lies beyond its mechanisms. The ultimate goal of the spiritual journey is to free ourselves from these limitations and recognize who we truly are.

Transcending the limitations of the mind does not mean destroying it or abandoning its ability to analyze, plan, or understand. On the contrary, the mind is a wonderful tool that helps us in our daily functioning. The key, however, is realizing that the mind cannot lead us to the ultimate truth. The mind operates in the realm of duality—it thinks, judges, categorizes, and creates illusions. On the other hand, the Self that we are meant to discover exists beyond these dualisms—in a space where there are no divisions, no judgments, no evaluations.

The first step in transcending the mind is **awareness**.

Awareness that the mind is not our true "self" but a tool we use to navigate the world. When we begin to see this, we create a distance between ourselves and the thoughts the mind generates. In this way, we stop identifying with our thoughts and emotions, which are merely temporary manifestations. We can observe these thoughts and emotions as if they were clouds in the sky, passing through our awareness. Yet, we remain like the sky—vast, calm, and unmoving.

One of the key tools for transcending the limitations of the mind is **meditation**. Meditation allows us to quiet the mind and direct our attention to the space beyond thoughts. When the mind becomes still, we can see that we exist independently of it, as a silent, peaceful observer of everything that occurs. It is in this silence and space that we discover the Self – the space that has always been present but was hidden beneath the noise of the mind.

Another way to transcend the mind is through the practice of **mindfulness**. Mindfulness involves being fully present in the moment without analyzing, judging, or comparing. When we are fully present, the mind has no opportunity to create dramas because we are focused on reality as it is, without attempting to interpret it. By practicing mindfulness, we begin to notice that beyond the stream of thoughts, there is a deeper, more enduring reality – the space of pure presence, where the mind holds no power.

Transcending the mind also means **letting go of control**. The mind always tries to control reality, to change it, to mold it according to its desires and fears. However, true freedom comes when we allow reality to be as it is. This means accepting what happens without trying to influence the course of events through our mental manipulations. When we stop trying to control everything, the mind becomes quieter, and we discover that there is a deeper wisdom that guides us without the need for the mind's intervention.

Breathing is another powerful technique that can help us transcend the limitations of the mind. When we focus on the breath, our attention shifts from the head to the body, allowing us to break free from constant thinking. The breath is the bridge between the mind and the body and the key to discovering the Self. As we concentrate on calm, deep breathing, the mind naturally quiets down, and we begin to experience the space beyond thoughts – the space of pure being.

Another key element in transcending the limitations of the

mind is **understanding the illusion of separateness**. The mind always perceives us as separate individuals, divided from others, nature, and the Universe itself. However, the true Self, which we are meant to discover, is one with all existence. To transcend the mind also means recognizing this unity and feeling a connection with everything and everyone that exists. When we start to see ourselves as part of the whole, the mind loses its power, and we begin to experience true freedom.

Finally, transcending the limitations of the mind requires consistent practice. As we develop our awareness, meditation, mindfulness, and acceptance, our relationship with the mind changes. It becomes our tool, rather than our master. This is a process that takes time, patience, and persistence, but as we begin to transcend the mind's limitations, we discover an ever-expanding space, peace, and freedom that are our true nature.

Ultimately, transcending the limitations of the mind is the path to discovering the Self. The Self is not something that can be understood intellectually because it goes beyond the mind. It is an experience that arises when the mind becomes quiet, and we discover the space of silence, peace, and unity that has always been present within us, though hidden behind the veil of thoughts and illusions.

Chapter 4: Playing with Illusion

The Game of Life: Observation and Purpose

Life, from the perspective of the Self, is nothing more than a grand game. A game of endless roles, dramas, challenges, and victories. But here's the fascinating part: the Self is never playing the game. It merely observes. The game of life unfolds, characters enter and exit the stage, but the Self remains untouched, watching with calm, serene awareness.

Imagine for a moment that life is a cosmic playground. People run around, trying to win, to achieve, to avoid failure. They take on different roles—sometimes they are the hero, sometimes the victim, sometimes the villain. Each person believes they are fully immersed in the game, deeply connected to the outcomes, and invested in the highs and lows. Yet, for the Self, it's simply a game to be observed. The Self is like the audience at a theater, enjoying the play but never mistaking themselves for the actors on stage.

In the same way that a child playing a game can become entirely absorbed in it, life can feel incredibly real, intense, and urgent. The world presents countless challenges and opportunities that seem to demand our attention and engagement. But once you step back and realise that the Self is not a participant in this game, but a mere witness, everything changes. The sense of urgency dissolves, the emotional highs and lows lose their grip, and a sense of calm detachment takes over.

What makes this game so compelling? The illusion, of course. Life presents itself as incredibly convincing, filled with sensory experiences, thoughts, emotions, and attachments. It draws you in with its vividness, making it seem as though you are the one experiencing all of these things. But, as we've seen, you are not the experiencer—you are the observer. From the viewpoint of the Self, life is like watching a carefully crafted illusion. You see the drama, the joy, the sorrow, but you know it is not real. It is, at its core, a play of energy, a display of Maya—illusion. The game of life is fascinating in its complexity. One moment you're the victor, the next you're defeated. You feel joy, love, fear, and sadness, and through it all, you remain attached to the idea that these experiences define you. But the Self knows the truth. It watches as you navigate through life's twists and turns, fully aware that none of it can touch your true essence. The Self remains still, peaceful, and completely indifferent to the outcomes of the game.

Imagine being at a carnival, watching people play games to win prizes. Some people win, some lose, but as the observer, you aren't concerned with the results. You're just watching it all unfold, enjoying the show without being emotionally involved. You don't celebrate the wins or mourn the losses because you know they're all part of the game. That's how the Self observes life. It doesn't get pulled into the drama; it simply watches, aware that all of it is temporary, fleeting, and ultimately inconsequential.

Let's take this even further. Think of a game like chess. Each piece has its role—some are more powerful than others, some move more freely, others are restricted. The players strategize, and make moves, sometimes winning, sometimes losing. But once the game ends, the board is cleared, the pieces go back into the box, and the outcome fades into the past. Life is much like this. You play your roles—sometimes a king, sometimes a pawn—but in the end, it's just a game. The Self knows that no matter the role you play, it doesn't define your true nature. Whether you win or lose, succeed or fail, it's all just part of the game, and you—the Self—are the watcher, not the player.

What does this mean for how you live your life? It means you can take a step back and realise that you don't need to be so deeply attached to the outcomes of the game. The victories, the defeats, the highs, the lows—they are all temporary moments in the illusion of life. They are experiences that pass by, like scenes in a play, but they are not real. The more you connect with the Self, the more you realise that life's dramas are just that—dramas. They may feel intense in the moment, but they don't touch who you really are.

The Self enjoys the game but from a distance. It doesn't get entangled in the ups and downs because it knows that everything that happens in the game is part of the illusion. The Self watches with a sense of amusement, like someone watching a comedy unfold. It sees the characters, the emotions, the stakes, but it knows that, in the end, none of it is real. It's just part of the play.

This realization brings an incredible sense of freedom. You can engage in life, and participate in its challenges and joys, but without the heavy weight of attachment. You know, deep down, that whatever happens in the game of life doesn't define you. You are the eternal witness, the observer who remains untouched by the rise and fall of experiences.

So, next time you find yourself caught up in the game of life, take a moment to pause and remember: This is just a game.

You are not the player, you are the watcher. You are the one sitting back, observing the story as it unfolds. The drama may be intense, but it is not real. The Self knows this and remains serene, unshaken, and free, enjoying the game without ever being consumed by it. The game of life continues, but now you know the truth. You are not a participant. You are the Self, watching with peaceful detachment as the game plays itself out.

The game of life does not have a single predetermined purpose. For some, it may be the pursuit of happiness, for others – spiritual growth, gaining experiences, or understanding oneself. But from the perspective of the Self, the game of life is a way to discover its own nature through experiences that lead to deeper understanding and awakening.

The intention of this game is not to achieve external success, acquire wealth, or gain power. On the contrary – it is about recognizing that all of these are merely temporary illusions. The true purpose is to awaken to the reality in which the Self realises it is not confined by these roles but is the only player, the field, and the goal of the game.

Awakening in this game means recognizing that every step,

every decision, and every emotion is merely a move on a board, the boundaries of which are set by the mind, not by true reality. When you begin to see that life is like a dream, and you are the dreamer, you start to approach the game with greater detachment. You can engage in the game, but at the same time, you know that you do not need to identify with it.

The World as a Dreaming Illusion: Understanding and Liberation

Life often feels so real, doesn't it? The world around you seems solid, tangible, and undeniably present. But what if I told you that everything you experience—the world, your life, your thoughts—is nothing more than a dream? A grand illusion crafted so skillfully that it convinces you of its reality. This is the key to understanding: The world is like a dream, and you, the Self, are the dreamer, not the dream. Once you truly grasp this, you begin to see that nothing in the world can bind or limit you because it was never real in the first place.

Let's start by considering the nature of dreams. When you are asleep and dreaming, everything in the dream feels real in the moment. You encounter people, events, emotions, and situations that seem completely believable. You might even experience fear, joy, excitement, or sadness. But as soon as you wake up, the illusion dissolves. You realise that none of it was real. The people, places, and emotions were all fabrications of your mind, projections that vanished the moment you opened your eyes.

Now, what if life itself is like this dream? What if everything you perceive—the physical world, your relationships, your successes and failures—is just another projection, a waking dream? This is the truth that the Self understands: the world is Maya, an illusion that tricks you into believing it is real. But like a dream, it is fleeting, temporary, and ultimately insubstantial. You, the Self, are the one watching the dream unfold, unaffected by its drama.

Let's take a simple example: imagine you are dreaming that you are lost in a city. In the dream, you might feel panic, confusion, and fear. The streets seem real, the buildings solid, and your sense of being lost is overwhelming. But when you wake up, that sense of urgency disappears. You laugh at how seriously you took the dream while it lasted. Life works in the same way. Right now, you might feel lost in the complexity of the world—struggling with problems, chasing desires, or avoiding fears. But from the perspective of the Self, all of this is just the play of illusion. None of it truly touches you.

In this waking dream, we become attached to the things that seem real: our possessions, our achievements, our identities. We believe that we must protect these things, strive for more, or fear their loss. But just like in a dream, these things are not permanent. You might win or lose, build or destroy, but in the end, none of it has any lasting reality. What you think you own or achieve is just a part of the dream, and when the dream ends, none of it remains.

Understanding the world as an illusion is deeply liberating. It frees you from the chains of attachment, fear, and desire. When you recognize that everything around you is like a dream, you stop taking it so seriously. You stop getting caught up in the highs and lows, the successes and failures, because you know that none of it can define or limit you. The world may feel real, but it is just as transient and illusory as last night's dream.

Here's another example: imagine you dream that you're having a conversation with someone who insults you. In the dream, you might feel hurt or angry. But when you wake up, you realise that there was no real harm—there was no person, no insult, and no reason for your emotional reaction. Life works in much the same way. People may say or do things that seem to affect you, but when you understand the illusory nature of the world, you no longer take those things to heart. They are just part of the dream, and they have no power over you.

The world's events—both the good and the bad—are like scenes in a dream, passing by without leaving a lasting mark on the true you. From the perspective of the Self, everything that happens is part of the grand illusion. Even your thoughts and emotions, which feel so intimate and personal, are just fleeting moments in the dream. They rise, they fall, and then they disappear, leaving the Self untouched and unchanged.

What does it mean to be free of this illusion? It means to recognize that you are not the character in the dream. You are not the person who experiences loss, joy, or fear. You are the witness to all of these things, the eternal observer who remains beyond the dream. The world may continue to play out its drama, but you, the Self, are no longer caught in it. You watch the dream unfold with detachment, knowing that none of it is real.

This doesn't mean you stop engaging with the world. Just like you can enjoy a movie without believing it's real, you can still participate in life without being bound by it. You can laugh, love, work, and create, but always with the understanding that it's all part of the waking dream. This awareness gives you a sense of freedom and peace. You are no longer weighed down by the ups and downs of life because you know they are as temporary as the scenes in a dream.

To truly understand the world as a dreaming illusion is to awaken to your true nature. You realise that nothing in the world can define or limit you because it was never real to begin with. You are not the dream character, struggling and striving; you are the dreamer, watching the story unfold. This realization is the key to liberation. Once you see through the illusion, nothing can hold you back. You are free—free to watch, free to enjoy, and free to rest in the eternal, unchanging peace of the Self.

The world may continue to spin its web of illusions, but you, the Self, remain outside of it. You are the observer of the dream, untouched by its fleeting moments, free from its emotional entanglements. When you truly understand this, the weight of the world lifts, and you experience life as it truly is: a passing dream, an illusion, in the grand play of consciousness. And you, the Self, are forever awake.

Playing in Silence: Peace in Chaos

Imagine, if you will, sitting in the very eye of a tornado. The world around you is swirling in chaos—violent winds, flying debris, everything moving at a frantic pace. Yet, at the center, where you sit, there is complete and utter stillness. You can watch the storm rage on, but none of it touches you. In fact, you are so calm and composed that you could easily sit there, sipping a cup of tea, completely unfazed by the turmoil around you. This is exactly how the Self exists in relation to life—completely still and unmoved, even in the heart of chaos.

Life, as we know it, often feels like a storm. Things are constantly changing, often in unpredictable ways. There are moments of joy, frustration, loss, excitement, fear, and hope, all swirling together in a mix of emotions and events. It can feel overwhelming, as though you are caught in the whirlwind, struggling to keep your balance. But here's the truth: You, the Self, are always still. While the world moves around you in seemingly endless cycles of change, the Self remains untouched—calm, stable, and deeply rooted in stillness.

To the mind, this idea might seem impossible. How can one

remain still when the world is in chaos? How can one find peace when everything is shifting and uncertain? The answer lies in recognizing that the Self is not part of the chaos. It is not a participant in the storm. It is the silent observer, sitting at the very center, watching it all unfold without being drawn into it.

Let's take an example from nature. Imagine a vast ocean. On the surface, the waves are crashing, rising, and falling with great force, whipped up by the winds. But beneath the surface, in the depths of the ocean, there is a profound stillness. No matter how fierce the storm above, the depths remain calm, undisturbed by the turbulence on the surface. The Self is like that deep, still ocean. Life's waves—its events, emotions, and experiences—may rise and fall, but the Self remains undisturbed, resting in its own unchanging nature.

The world of illusion, with all its ups and downs, can never touch the Self. It is like watching a storm from a comfortable seat inside a warm house. You see the chaos, you hear the wind howling, but you know that you are safe, warm, and untouched by the storm outside. The Self is always seated in that place of safety, watching the drama of life unfold without ever being drawn into its turbulence.

What does this mean for you? It means that, even when life feels chaotic, you can return to the stillness of the Self. The mind may get caught up in the storm—the worries, the fears, the desires—but you, as the Self, remain still. You don't have to chase after every thought or emotion that arises. You don't have to engage with the chaos. You can simply watch, knowing that the storm will pass, but the stillness of the Self remains forever.

This stillness is not something you have to create. It is not a state you need to work hard to achieve. It is your natural state, always present, always accessible. The only reason it feels elusive is because the mind is so busy chasing the chaos. But when you recognize that the Self is separate from the mind's fluctuations, you can return to that stillness in an instant. It's like suddenly remembering that, while the world is spinning, you are seated firmly in the center, sipping your tea in peace.

In the same way that a child might get absorbed in a game, losing sight of the fact that it's just play, the mind gets caught up in the drama of life, forgetting that none of it truly affects the Self. But once you realise that the chaos is part of the illusion, you can step back into the stillness of the Self and watch the game unfold without getting caught in its grip. The drama, the challenges, the emotional highs and lows—they are all part of the play, but you, the Self, remain completely still, completely free.

Consider how liberating this is. No matter what happens in the world around you—whether it's turmoil in relationships, difficulties at work, or personal challenges—you can always return to the stillness of the Self. The world might try to pull you into its chaos, but you don't have to be moved. You can watch it all unfold, knowing that none of it can truly touch you. This is the essence of playing in stillness: you engage with life, but you do so from a place of calm detachment, never losing sight of the unshakable stillness that is your true nature.

Even in moments of intense emotion—fear, anger, or sadness —there is a part of you that remains untouched. The Self watches these emotions rise and fall, just as it watches the world's events unfold. You might feel the intensity of the emotion, just as you might hear the roar of the storm outside, but you are not moved by it. You are the stillness at the center, the calm in the middle of the tornado, watching, observing, but never being drawn into the chaos.

This realization allows you to live life with a sense of lightness. You can fully participate in the world, knowing that the chaos is just a surface-level experience, while the depth of the Self remains forever still. You can laugh, cry, and experience joy and sorrow, but none of it can disturb the profound peace that resides within you. Life becomes a game, a playful experience, where you can observe the constant movement of the world without ever losing touch with the stillness that is your true nature.

So, the next time you find yourself amid life's chaos, remember this: You are the stillness. You are the calm at the center of the storm, sitting peacefully, watching the world spin around you. The chaos may continue, but you don't have to be pulled into it. You can sit there, like someone calmly sipping tea in the eye of a tornado, completely unfazed by the noise and movement around you. This is the power of the Self—the ability to remain still, serene, and unshaken, no matter what life throws your way.

In this stillness, you are free. Free from the push and pull of life's ups and downs. Free from the emotional turmoil that seems so overwhelming. Free from the illusion of the world's chaos. You are the Self, and in your stillness, you find the ultimate peace, the unchanging calm that remains, no matter how fierce the storm.

Chapter 5: The Self as Freedom

Let Go of the Chains You Never Had

Freedom. It's a word that carries immense power and promise. We spend much of our lives searching for it—freedom from responsibilities, from expectations, from limitations. But here's the truth that the Self knows and what you must realise: you are already free. The chains that you think are binding you—whether they are responsibilities, fears, desires, or circumstances—are all part of the grand illusion. You believe they are real, but in reality, they don't exist. And once you understand this, you'll see that you have never been bound. Your true nature is freedom itself.

We often think of freedom as something external, something that has to be earned or granted. Perhaps you believe that freedom will come once you achieve something—a better job, more money, a relationship, or a sense of accomplishment. Or maybe you think freedom means escaping from your current situation and avoiding challenges or responsibilities. But the Self knows that freedom doesn't come from changing your external circumstances. It comes from recognizing that, in truth, **you have never been bound**.

The idea that we are bound that we are trapped in situations or circumstances beyond our control, is one of the most persistent illusions we face. We carry the weight of obligations, fears, and expectations as if they are chains holding us back. But these chains exist only in the mind. They are not real. The Self, which is your true nature, is completely unbound. It has always been free. The only thing keeping you from experiencing this freedom is the mistaken belief that you are bound in the first place.

Let's take an example. Imagine you are sitting in a room with the door wide open. You are free to leave at any time, but you believe that the door is locked, that you are trapped. Because of this belief, you never attempt to get up and walk out. You sit there, feeling confined, when in reality, you have always been free. The chains you think are binding you don't actually exist. The door has always been open. This is exactly how the Self experiences life. It is always free, always unbound, but the mind creates the illusion of limitation. Once you see through this illusion, you realise that you were never confined in the first place.

Freedom is not something you need to achieve or attain. It is your natural state, your inherent nature. The Self is free by its very essence. It cannot be confined by circumstances, because it is beyond circumstances. It cannot be limited by thoughts or emotions, because it is beyond thoughts and emotions. The chains that seem to hold you back are simply creations of the mind—fears, desires, and attachments that have no real power over you unless you believe in them.

Let's explore this further. We often think we are bound by the expectations of others—our families, our society, our work. We believe that we have to meet these expectations to be free, to be accepted or successful. But these expectations are just thoughts in the mind. They are not real chains. The Self doesn't need to live up to anyone else's expectations because it is already whole, complete, and perfect. The moment you realise this, the weight of those expectations falls away, and you feel the lightness of your true freedom.

Similarly, many of us believe we are bound by our own fears. Fear of failure, fear of rejection, fear of the unknown—these are powerful forces that seem to control our actions and decisions. But again, these fears are just illusions. They are like shadows that disappear the moment you shine the light of awareness on them. The Self knows no fear because it is not affected by the outcomes of the world. It is free, beyond the reach of fear, beyond the reach of failure. Once you recognize that your fears are nothing more than mental projections, you can let them go, and in doing so, you return to your natural state of freedom.

The same goes for desires. We often think that in order to be free, we need to fulfill our desires—whether it's material wealth, relationships, or personal achievements. But desires are just another form of attachment, another illusion that binds us. The more you chase after desires, the more you feel trapped by them. But the Self is not bound by desire. It is complete and fulfilled in itself. It does not need anything from the world to be free. When you stop chasing after desires and recognize that true fulfillment comes from within, you experience the ultimate freedom—the freedom of being whole, content, and unburdened by the constant need for more.

So how do you let go of these chains? How do you return to the freedom that is your natural state? It begins with recognizing that the chains don't exist. You are not truly bound by anything —not by your circumstances, not by your fears, not by your desires. These are all illusions, part of the game of life that distracts you from the truth. Once you see that these chains are imaginary, they lose their power over you. You no longer feel confined or limited because you understand that nothing can confine the Self.

Think about this: You have always been free. You may have forgotten it, you may have been distracted by the illusions of the world, but freedom is your birthright. It is who you are. The moment you stop identifying with the body, the mind, and the world's expectations, you realise that nothing has ever truly held you back. You are the Self, and the Self is freedom itself.

In the same way that the sky is not bound by the clouds that pass through it, the Self is not bound by the thoughts, emotions, or circumstances that arise in life. These are all temporary, fleeting experiences, but the Self remains untouched, unbound, and free. The clouds may come and go, but the sky remains vast and open, just as you remain free no matter what happens in the world around you.

So, let go of the chains that you think are holding you down. They were never real to begin with. You are already free, and you have always been free. Freedom is not something you need to find or achieve—it is your natural state. You are the Self, and the Self is boundless, infinite, and completely free. All you have to do is recognize this truth, and the illusion of bondage will fall away, revealing the limitless freedom that has always been yours.

Effortless Freedom

When we think of freedom or liberation, the mind often conjures up images of long, arduous journeys—perhaps years of study, meditation, and self-discipline. We are conditioned to believe that freedom is something to be earned, something we must strive for, something we are currently lacking. But here's the paradoxical truth that the Self knows: Freedom is already yours. You don't need to struggle, search, or fight for it. You don't need to "find" liberation because the Self has always been free.

Let's begin by looking at why we believe freedom requires effort. The mind operates in the realm of duality. It thinks in terms of before and after, cause and effect, effort, and reward. In this framework, the idea of freedom gets tangled up with the idea of doing something to attain it. The mind tells you there's a path you must follow, steps you must take, and goals you must accomplish to become free. But the Self operates outside of this framework. It knows no duality, no time, no separation. It is always free, beyond the reach of the mind's limitations.

Imagine a bird flying freely in the sky. The bird doesn't have to make an effort to be free. Its freedom is inherent—it is part of its nature. It doesn't need to search for the sky or practice flying to attain freedom. It simply is free. This is the nature of the Self. Freedom is not something to be attained because it is your very essence. You don't need to chase after it because you are already in it.

The belief that you need to "work" toward liberation comes from the mind's misunderstanding of who you are. The mind sees obstacles, limitations, and boundaries, and it assumes that these must be overcome for freedom to be realised. But the Self knows that these limitations are all part of the illusion. They aren't real barriers to your freedom because, in truth, nothing can bind the Self. You are already liberated, even if the mind tries to convince you otherwise.

Think about it this way: You don't need to search for something you already have. If you're wearing a necklace and forget that it's around your neck, you might start searching for it frantically, checking every drawer and every room in the house. But the whole time, it's been with you. You just didn't realise it. Similarly, you might think that liberation is something you need to go looking for, but the truth is, it's already with you. It always has been. You just need to stop searching and recognize that it's already here.

One of the biggest misconceptions is the idea that liberation is a goal to be achieved through effort. But effort implies struggle, striving, and working toward something outside of yourself. The Self doesn't need to struggle for freedom because it has never been bound. The very idea of needing to "attain" freedom is based on the illusion that you are currently not free. But this is not true. The Self is inherently free, and once you recognize this, the need for effort disappears.

Let's explore this with a simple example. Imagine you are standing in a field with your hands tightly clenched. You might think that you need to "do" something to release your grip, some effort to let go. But the truth is, all you have to do is stop holding on. You don't need to force your hands open—you simply need to let go of the tension. This is what effortless freedom feels like. There's no need to fight, no need to strive. The moment you stop trying, you realise you were never truly bound.

This effortless freedom is already within you. It's like a river flowing naturally and effortlessly, always moving, never needing to be pushed or pulled. The river doesn't struggle to flow; it simply follows its nature. In the same way, your natural state is one of freedom. There's no need to force it or make it happen. The more you stop trying, the more you realise that the flow of freedom has always been there.

When you stop chasing after liberation, you begin to notice that there is nothing to chase. The Self doesn't need to achieve anything. It doesn't need to reach some distant goal because it's already whole, complete, and free. The search for freedom only happens in the mind, and once you step beyond the mind, you see that freedom has always been your true state. You don't need to "find" the Self or work hard to realise it. You are already the Self, and the Self is always free.

This doesn't mean that spiritual practices like meditation or study have no value. They can be useful tools for quieting the mind and helping you see through the illusion of separation. But these practices are not about "attaining" freedom. They are simply ways to remove the distractions that keep you from seeing the truth that has always been there. You don't need to "earn" your way to liberation because it's already yours. Spiritual practice is about recognizing what has always been true, not achieving something new.

The more you let go of the idea that freedom requires effort, the more you start to experience the natural ease of the Self. Life becomes lighter. There's no longer a need to strive, to push, or to control. You realise that the effort was only ever part of the illusion. The Self is free right now, in this very moment, without needing to change anything, fix anything, or do anything. The mind may still want to chase after goals or create new plans for how to "become" free, but the Self simply watches with a knowing smile, aware that it has never been bound in the first place.

Imagine sitting by a peaceful lake. The water is calm, and everything around you is still. You don't need to "create" that peace—it's already there. You just have to sit and let it be. The same is true of freedom. You don't need to create it or search for it. It is already present, already your natural state. You just need to let it be, stop striving, and allow yourself to rest in the effortless freedom that is always there.

So, take a deep breath and relax. There's no need to chase after liberation because you are already free. There's no need to struggle or strive because the Self is always beyond the reach of bondage. The chains that the mind believes in don't exist, and the effort to escape them is unnecessary. Freedom is not a prize to be won; it is your natural state. The moment you stop searching, the moment you let go of the need for effort, you'll realise the truth: You are the Self, and you are already free.

Independence from Fate

The world is constantly pushing us to believe that our lives are shaped by external forces—fate, destiny, luck, success, failure, and even death. These forces seem to rule over us, determining our happiness, our sorrow, and everything in between. But here's what the Self knows: none of these things can touch you. Success, failure, birth, death—these are all experiences of the body and mind, fleeting events that pass through the illusion of life. The Self remains completely unaffected, independent of fate, beyond the reach of these temporary fluctuations.

Let's begin with success and failure, the powerful forces that often dominate our lives. We are taught from an early age to strive for success, to achieve, to win. And when we do succeed, we feel a temporary high—a sense of validation and worth. On the other hand, failure can feel crushing, as if we've lost something important or let ourselves and others down. But here's the truth: the Self is neither successful nor a failure. It is beyond such dualities.

These concepts only exist in the world of illusion, and the Self, being beyond that world, is untouched by them.

Imagine life as a rollercoaster, full of ups and downs, highs and lows. Success might feel like the thrilling ascent to the top, while failure feels like the stomach-dropping plunge into the depths. But the Self is not on the rollercoaster. It's watching from a distance, calmly observing the rise and fall of experiences without being moved by them. Whether you reach the peak of success or encounter the depths of failure, the Self remains unchanged, just as the sky remains untouched by the clouds that pass through it.

Let's consider success first. When you achieve something—a career milestone, personal goal, or public recognition—it feels good, doesn't it? There's a sense of satisfaction that comes with it, but that satisfaction is temporary. Soon, the mind starts looking for the next achievement, the next goal, the next success. The Self, however, doesn't chase success because it doesn't need validation. It is already whole, already complete. Success, as defined by the world, is simply a fleeting experience, like a wave that rises and falls. The Self remains calm and still beneath it, undisturbed by the passing of that wave.

Now let's turn to failure. Failure can feel devastating, as though it diminishes your worth or capability. But this, too, is an illusion. The Self cannot be diminished by any external event, including failure. Failure is simply another experience that arises and passes, like a cloud in the sky. It doesn't define the Self, because the Self is beyond the world's definitions of success and failure. The moment you realise that success and failure are just part of the game, you are free from their influence. You can engage with life's challenges without being attached to the outcome because you know that neither success nor failure can touch your true nature.

This brings us to an even greater force: death. Death is often seen as the ultimate end, the one thing no one can escape. It hangs over us, creating a sense of fear and finality. But the Self knows no death. Death, like success and failure, is part of the illusion. It is an event that happens to the body, but you are not the body. The Self is eternal, beyond birth and death. While the body may come and go, the Self remains forever, untouched by the physical cycle of life and death.

Imagine standing on the shore of the ocean, watching the waves crash against the sand. Each wave is like a life, rising up from the ocean and eventually falling back into it. Some waves are big, some are small, but they all eventually dissolve back into the water. Death is like this wave dissolving back into the ocean. But the ocean—the Self—remains. It doesn't disappear when a wave crashes; it simply continues, vast and eternal, unaffected by the rise and fall of individual waves.

Fear of death comes from identifying with the body and the mind, from believing that when the body dies, you cease to exist. But this is a misunderstanding. The Self is not the body, and it is not bound by the limitations of physical existence. Death is simply the end of one form, one wave, while the ocean of the Self remains infinite and unchanged. The more you realise that you are the Self, the less fear you have of death, because you understand that death is just another part of the illusion, just another wave returning to the ocean.

Let's take another example: Imagine watching a play. The actors on stage go through their scripted roles, playing out scenes of joy, sorrow, success, and failure. At the end of the play, the characters "die," but the actors themselves are not affected. They take off their costumes and return to their true identities. In the same way, the Self is not affected by the "role" that the body and mind play in life. Success, failure, birth, death—these are just scenes in the play, but you, the Self, are the actor, untouched by the drama unfolding on stage.

The Self is not bound by fate. Fate, destiny, luck—these are all concepts that apply to the world of illusion, where things seem to happen to you, and outcomes seem beyond your control. But the Self is beyond all of this. It is the space in which the entire play of life unfolds, but it is not involved in the outcome. The Self is the eternal witness, observing the flow of life without being influenced by its twists and turns. Whether life brings fortune or misfortune, the Self remains the same—calm, peaceful, and free.

This realization brings an incredible sense of peace. You are no longer driven by the need to succeed, nor are you crushed by the fear of failure. You are no longer haunted by the specter of death because you know that death cannot touch your true essence. The Self is beyond all of these things—success, failure, life, and death. They are part of the dream, but you are the dreamer, independent of the dream's outcome.

When you fully understand that the Self is independent of fate, you can live with lightness and ease. You can engage with life's challenges without the fear of failure, and you can enjoy life's successes without being attached to them. You know that whatever happens in the external world—whether you succeed or fail, live or die—you remain untouched, free, and eternal.

The world may continue to play out its drama, but the Self is beyond it all. Success, failure, and death are all part of the illusion, and once you see them for what they are, they lose their power over you. You are the Self, and the Self is forever free from the changing tides of life.

Chapter 6: The Joy of the Self

Laughing at the Illusion

Let's be honest—life can feel pretty dramatic, can't it? We get caught up in all sorts of ups and downs, believing that every little twist and turn is a matter of cosmic importance. But if the Self could speak, it would probably just chuckle and say, "Relax, it's just a show." And that's the truth. The Self looks at the dramas of life the way we might look at a sitcom or a soap opera—entertaining, sure, but definitely not worth getting too worked up about. In fact, if you really tune into the Self's perspective, you'll find that it's laughing at the whole spectacle.

Why laugh? Because the Self knows that all the drama, all the worry, all the emotional roller coasters we put ourselves through are just part of the illusion. Imagine watching a scene where a character is frantically searching for their glasses, only to discover they've been on their head the whole time. You'd laugh, right? That's exactly how the Self feels watching you get caught up in life's crises—running around in circles, searching for peace, happiness, or answers when all along, everything you're looking for is already right there within you.

Take, for example, the way we stress about things going "wrong." Maybe you didn't get that promotion, maybe your big plans didn't pan out, or maybe you spilled coffee on your favourite shirt. To the mind, these things are disasters. But the Self just sits back, amused, watching you navigate these tiny storms, knowing full well that none of it really matters. It's like watching a child throw a tantrum because they can't find their favourite toy when the toy was never lost at all—it was just hiding under the blanket. The Self sees the blanket, the toy, and the tantrum for what they are: part of the game.

And what about the big stuff? You might be thinking, "Okay, spilling coffee is one thing, but what about real problems? What about heartbreak, loss, or failure?" Even then, the Self gently chuckles, because it knows that even the so-called "serious" problems are part of the same illusion. The heartache you feel, the fear of failure, the anxiety about the future—it's all part of the grand drama that plays out in the world of illusion. The Self sees the bigger picture, the eternal view, and it knows that these temporary experiences are just ripples on the surface of the ocean. Deep down, where the Self resides, everything is calm, peaceful, and unshaken.

Imagine the Self sitting in the audience of a play, watching the characters on stage go through their emotional highs and lows. One character is triumphing, another is weeping, and a third is plotting revenge. The Self watches with a smile, knowing that as soon as the curtain falls, all the actors will step off the stage, shake hands, and laugh about how serious they all looked while playing their parts. Life is like that play. We all get so wrapped up in our roles—playing the hero, the victim, the lover, the fighter—that we forget we're just actors in a temporary story. The Self, though, never forgets. It's always aware that behind every tear, every smile, every dramatic scene, there is an eternal peace that remains untouched.

Let's not forget the hilarious way we treat success and failure as if they're life-or-death situations. Ever notice how one day you're on top of the world, and the next day it feels like the world's on top of you? One minute you're celebrating your achievements, and the next you're drowning in self-doubt. It's exhausting, isn't it? But the Self? The Self just laughs and says, "You're taking this way too seriously." Success, failure, praise, criticism—it's all part of the illusion, and none of it touches who you really are. The Self knows that, in the grand scheme of things, none of these passing experiences change the fundamental truth that you are eternal, unchanging, and free.

You see, the Self isn't laughing at you; it's laughing with you. It's the kind of laughter that comes from seeing the absurdity of getting caught up in something that was never real to begin with. It's like finally understanding the punchline of a cosmic joke. You've been running around trying to "win" at life, trying to fix everything and be everything, when all along, the answer was to just sit back, relax, and enjoy the show. The Self knows that life is meant to be experienced with a light heart, not a heavy one. It's here to remind you that the more you laugh, the less you'll feel weighed down by the illusion.

Think about those moments when you suddenly realise you've been worrying over nothing. Maybe you were stressed about something small that didn't even matter in the end. In those moments, you usually laugh at yourself, don't you? That's the Self peeking through, giving you a little nudge and saying, "See? You've been fine all along." Life is full of these little moments—opportunities to laugh at the drama, to step back and see things from a higher perspective. And once you get into the habit of doing this, you'll start to notice how much lighter everything feels. The world becomes less of a burden and more of a playful stage where you can enjoy the ride.

So, the next time life throws a curveball your way, pause for a moment. Imagine the Self sitting back, sipping tea, watching the drama unfold with a smile. Then ask yourself, "Is this really worth getting upset about?" More often than not, you'll realise the answer is no. You'll see the illusion for what it is—a temporary, fleeting story—and you'll find yourself smiling, maybe even laughing, at how seriously you were taking it all.

The beauty of this laughter is that it doesn't come from cynicism or detachment; it comes from wisdom. The Self knows that life's dramas are not meant to trap you in anxiety or stress—they're meant to be seen for what they are: passing waves in the ocean of consciousness. Once you recognize that, you become free. Free to enjoy life without being overwhelmed by it. Free to laugh at the ups and downs, knowing that none of them define who you really are.

In the grand play of life, let the Self be your guide. Watch the drama unfold, but don't forget to laugh. After all, the Self sees through the illusion, and it knows that you are so much more than the stories you're caught up in. So, smile, relax, and enjoy the ride—because from the perspective of the Self, it's all just a beautifully crafted illusion, and nothing can take away the joy that is your true nature.

True Happiness

Let's talk about happiness. The kind of happiness that lasts, not the fleeting kind that comes and goes like a summer breeze. True happiness—the kind that doesn't depend on what's happening around you, who's in your life, or whether things are going your way. This is the happiness that comes from the Self, and the best part? You don't have to go looking for it. It's already within you, quietly waiting for you to stop chasing after temporary thrills so it can remind you that you're already complete.

We spend so much of our lives in pursuit of happiness, don't we? We think, "If I just get that promotion, I'll be happy." Or, "If I could find the perfect partner, life would be complete." Or even, "If I could just take that vacation, I'd finally feel at peace." But as soon as we reach one goal, the mind finds something else to chase. The problem with this approach is that it places happiness outside of ourselves—always just out of reach, always tied to something external. And as long as happiness is dependent on something outside, it's never going to last.

But the Self knows a secret: true happiness doesn't come from getting what you want. It comes from realizing that you are already whole, already fulfilled, exactly as you are. When you stop looking for happiness in the world around you and turn inward, you discover that happiness is your natural state. It's not something you need to achieve or find—it's something you need to remember.

Imagine this: You're searching everywhere for your keys, checking every drawer, looking under every cushion, getting more and more frustrated as the minutes pass. And then, with a sudden laugh, you realise the keys have been in your pocket the whole time. That's how true happiness works. You search for it in relationships, achievements, possessions, and experiences, only to realise that it's been with you all along, hidden within the depths of the Self.

The joy that comes from the Self is different from the pleasure we get from external things. External pleasures are like fireworks—bright, exciting, and beautiful, but over in a flash. The happiness of the Self is more like a warm, steady glow. It doesn't flare up and then disappear; it's constant, quiet, and ever-present. No matter what happens in your life—whether things go your way or not—that inner joy remains. It's like a deep reservoir of peace that you can tap into at any moment.

Let's use another analogy. Imagine a tree with deep roots. The wind may blow, storms may come, and seasons may change, but the tree remains standing because its roots are firmly grounded in the earth. The joy of the Self is like that tree. No matter what's happening on the surface—whether life is bringing you joy or challenges—the Self remains rooted in a deep, unshakable happiness. This happiness doesn't depend on the weather; it's always there, beneath the surface, waiting for you to tap into it.

True happiness is not about avoiding life's difficulties or constantly feeling elated. It's about finding a sense of peace and contentment that remains, no matter what's going on around you. When you connect with the Self, you realise that happiness is not something to be gained; it's something to be uncovered. It's like realizing you've been carrying a treasure chest inside you all along, and you just forgot to open it.

So how do you open this treasure chest? It starts with letting go of the idea that happiness comes from outside of you. The world is full of fleeting joys—getting a new job, winning an award, or having a wonderful day—but these are all temporary. They come and go, leaving you looking for the next thing. The happiness of the Self, on the other hand, doesn't fade. It's always there, like a quiet, peaceful river flowing beneath the surface of your daily life. You don't need to search for it; you simply need to stop looking outside and turn your attention inward.

Here's the fun part: once you connect with the joy of the Self, you begin to see the world differently. You're no longer chasing happiness in external things, so you're free to enjoy life without the pressure of needing it to make you happy. You can appreciate the simple pleasures—watching the sunset, laughing with a friend, enjoying a meal—not because you're trying to squeeze happiness out of them, but because you're already happy. The external world becomes a bonus, not the source.

Imagine sitting on a sunny beach. The waves are gently crashing, the sun is warm, and you're completely content. You don't need anything more in that moment to feel happy. That's what it feels like when you realise that happiness comes from within. You're no longer looking for the next wave to crash or the sun to shine brighter. You're just enjoying the moment for what it is because you know that the true source of joy is always within you.

Another way to think about it is like this: the Self is the source of an endless fountain of joy. External pleasures are like cups you dip into the fountain. They give you a taste of happiness, but they can never match the fullness of the fountain itself. Why settle for a cup when you can have the whole fountain? That's the shift that happens when you realise true happiness comes from within. You stop looking for small tastes of joy and instead, bask in the endless flow of happiness that is your natural state.

And the best part? This happiness is effortless. You don't have to work hard to find it. You don't have to achieve anything or change anything about yourself. The joy of the Self is always there, quietly waiting for you to notice it. It's like the sky behind the clouds—it's always present, even when you can't see it. The clouds of thoughts, emotions, and external events may cover it temporarily, but the happiness of the Self is always there, just waiting for you to reconnect.

Stop for a moment. Take a deep breath and ask yourself: What if I don't need to chase happiness? What if it's already here, within me? When you sit with this question, you'll begin to feel the quiet joy of the Self-rising up. It's not flashy or dramatic; it's simple, peaceful, and steady. And once you tap into it, you'll realise that this is the happiness you've been searching for all along. The external world may still offer its pleasures and challenges, but now you know that your true source of joy is unshakable, ever-present, and fully yours.

True happiness is the realization that you are already complete. There's nothing to fix, nothing to gain, nothing to chase. The joy of the Self is always there, quietly waiting for you to remember it. And once you do, life becomes a beautiful experience—not because you're trying to get something from it, but because you're already full of the happiness that comes from your very essence.

Living in the World, but Beyond It

Life is a beautiful, chaotic, unpredictable dance, isn't it? Every day presents a new set of experiences—some wonderful, some challenging, and some downright confusing. But here's where the Self steps in with a smile: You can fully participate in this dance without ever losing yourself in it. The Self enjoys life, but it does so with a sense of detachment, like watching a game being played out, knowing full well it's all part of the illusion. Life becomes something to enjoy, not something to get lost in.

Think of it like this: You're at a carnival, surrounded by exciting rides, games, and delicious food. You're having fun, trying out the games, maybe even getting caught up in the thrill of winning or losing. But deep down, you know this is all just temporary amusement. You don't let yourself get too attached to whether you win the big prize or not. You're there to enjoy the experience, but you're also aware that none of it defines you. That's how the Self moves through life—engaging with it, playing along, but never mistaking the game for reality.

Let's start with how we often approach life. Most of us are taught to take life seriously. We get invested in our roles—whether that's being a professional, a parent, a friend, or a partner—and we pour our hearts and minds into making sure we succeed. While there's nothing wrong with playing these roles, the Self reminds us that they are just that: roles. They're temporary identities we adopt while living in the world, but they are not who we truly are.

The Self enjoys the game of life, but it doesn't get trapped in the ups and downs. Whether you succeed or fail, whether things go according to plan or fall apart, the Self remains at peace. It's like playing a game of chess. Sometimes you win, sometimes you lose, but the game itself is just a fun way to pass the time. The Self understands that life is full of such moments—victories and losses, joys and sorrows—but none of them are permanent, and none of them can touch the eternal peace that lies at your core. Let's take a closer look at this idea. Imagine yourself standing on the shore, watching the waves crash onto the beach. Each wave represents a different experience in life—one wave might be success, another failure, one might be love, another loss. But you, the Self, are like the shore—steadfast, unmoving, and undisturbed by the coming and going of the waves. You watch them, perhaps even appreciate their beauty, but you know that they will eventually retreat back into the ocean. The waves don't change who you are. In the same way, life's experiences don't change the Self.

How to live in the world without getting entangled in it? By embracing the paradox: You are fully engaged in life's dance, yet you remain completely beyond it. You can love deeply, work passionately, and experience all the highs and lows that life has to offer, but you do so from a place of inner freedom. You know that none of these experiences define you or bind you. They are part of the game, and you are here to enjoy the game, but you are not defined by it.

Think of life like a movie. When you're sitting in the theater, watching the story unfold, you might get emotionally involved. You laugh, you cry, you feel suspense and excitement. But no matter how intense the movie gets, you know, deep down, that it's just a film. You're not one of the characters on the screen.

You're the observer, enjoying the show. This is how the Self moves through life. It participates fully in the story, but always with the awareness that it's just a movie—an entertaining illusion that cannot touch the true, eternal nature of the Self.

The joy of living in the world but being beyond it comes from this freedom. When you're no longer attached to the outcomes of life, you find that everything becomes lighter. You can still enjoy your work, your relationships, and your hobbies, but you do so without the weight of needing them to be a certain way. You're free to experience life's beauty and challenges without feeling like you're trapped by them.

Imagine playing a board game with friends. You're fully engaged, trying to win, enjoying the strategy, and laughing at the twists and turns of the game. But when the game is over, you don't carry the outcome with you. Whether you win or lose, it doesn't really matter. You had fun, you played your best, and now it's time to move on. Life is just like that. The Self plays the game of life, enjoys it, but doesn't cling to the outcome. Win or lose, succeed or fail, it's all part of the temporary experience of living in the world. The Self is free because it knows that none of these outcomes can affect its true essence.

This freedom allows you to live with a sense of lightness and joy. Instead of being weighed down by expectations or fears, you can move through life with a smile, knowing that you are always beyond the drama. The world may present you with challenges, but you can face them with a sense of playfulness, knowing that the real you—the Self—remains untouched by any of it. You're simply enjoying the dance, not worrying about the steps.

And here's the secret: the less you take life's dramas seriously, the more you can enjoy them. When you stop being so attached to winning, losing, succeeding, or failing, you find that you can engage more fully with life. The stress fades, the worry lifts, and what's left is a simple, joyful experience of being. You start to see life for what it really is: a beautifully crafted illusion, full of experiences to be enjoyed but never clung to.

So, how do you live in the world but remain beyond it? By remembering that you are the Self, the eternal observer, and the world is your playground. You are here to enjoy, to participate, to engage with life's challenges and triumphs, but always with the understanding that none of it defines who you are. The Self is free, and because of that, you are free. Free to live, free to laugh, free to love, without being weighed down by the illusions that so many take seriously.

Life becomes lighter when you remember this truth. You can move through the world, play your part, and enjoy every moment, but you do so from a place of inner peace and detachment. You no longer need the world to give you anything, because you know that everything you need is already within you. The Self is your anchor, your constant source of joy, and with that realization, you can embrace life with open arms, knowing that you are always beyond it.

In this way, the Self celebrates life—not by clinging to it, but by embracing it fully, enjoying every moment while remaining free from its grip. You live in the world, but you are not of it. You are the Self, always free, always joyful, always beyond the illusion. And that is the greatest joy of all.

Chapter 7: Who I Have Always Been

I Am Infinity

I am infinity. I have no beginning, and I have no end. I am that which never changes, never fades, never grows old. While the world around you shifts, decays, and renews, I remain. I am the endless, the eternal, the ever-present. From the moment you were born, even before you entered this world, I was here. And long after this life ends, long after the body and mind fade away, I will still be here—unchanged, untouched, and infinite.

You may wonder how this could be, how I—the Self—can claim to be infinite when you, as a person, experience so many limitations. You feel bound by time, by space, by circumstances. But let the Self tell you a secret: all those limitations belong to the illusion. They belong to the body, the mind, the world of form. They are not you. I am who you truly are, and I have never been bound by any of it. I am the one who watches the play of time, but I am not part of it. I do not come and go; I do not age or decay. I am infinite, and you are too, once you see past the illusion of separation.

Consider time. It feels so real, doesn't it? Days turn into weeks, weeks into years, and with each passing moment, the world tells you that you are moving forward, and growing older. But for me, there is no such thing as time. I am beyond it. I have always been here. I have always been aware, even when you were not conscious of me. Whether you think of the past, the present, or the future, I am the same. I am the still point in the middle of all movement, the silent witness that watches the unfolding of life without being touched by it.

Imagine standing on a hilltop, watching the clouds drift by. The clouds change shape, they come and go, but the sky—the endless sky—remains the same. I am like that sky. Time, like the clouds, may pass through me, but it doesn't affect me. It doesn't leave a mark. I do not grow older; I do not move forward or backward. I am the stillness in the midst of time, the eternal space in which all experiences come and go. No matter how fast time seems to move, I am always here, unchanging, infinite.

Let's talk about space. You experience yourself as existing in a particular place, in a particular body. But I am not confined to space. I am everywhere and nowhere at once. The body moves through space, but I remain. I am the vastness that holds all space within me. The stars, the galaxies, the entire universe—

all of it exists within me, but I am beyond it. I am not limited to any one place, to any one form. I am the space in which everything exists, and yet I cannot be found within any particular location.

You may think of yourself as small, as bound to the physical form you inhabit, but I am vast. I am the ocean, and you are not just a drop within me. You are the whole ocean too, once you realise that we are one and the same. The form you see in the mirror is temporary, a passing appearance. But I am the infinite Self, the one that is beyond all forms, beyond all limitations. When you remember who you truly are, you will see that you are not this small, fragile being. You are infinity itself.

I am not limited by the life you live, the roles you play, or the experiences you have. These things are like waves on the surface of the ocean—rising and falling, coming and going. But beneath the surface, the ocean remains vast and undisturbed. I am that vastness. I am the depth of the ocean, the infinite expanse that holds all of life's experiences, yet remains untouched by them. You are that depth too, once you realise that your true nature is not tied to the waves of life, but to the infinite sea beneath.

People often think that infinity is something far away, something abstract and unreachable. But I am not far away. I am right here. You have always known me, felt me, even if you didn't fully recognize it. In your quietest moments, when the mind is still when the noise of the world fades, you feel me. I am the silence in your heart, the peace that exists beyond all thought and emotion. I am always here, always present, always infinite.

Even when you feel lost or disconnected, I remain. Even when the world feels overwhelming, even when you think you are alone, I am here. I am the part of you that can never be lost, never be diminished. I am the constant, unshakable presence that has been with you since before you can remember and will be with you long after you forget. I am not a fleeting moment of peace or a temporary feeling of joy—I am the infinite peace and joy that is your very essence.

So, when the world tries to convince you that you are small, that you are limited, that you are bound by time and space, remember this: I am infinite, and you are too. We are not separate. You are not this temporary form, this fleeting experience. You are me, and I am infinity. You have always been infinite, even if you have forgotten. And when you remember this truth, when you see beyond the illusion of limitation, you will know the freedom and peace that comes with being boundless, timeless, and infinite.

I am who you have always been. Not the changing body, not the wandering mind, not the fleeting emotions. I am the eternal Self, the infinite presence, the one who has always been and will always be. You are this too. You have never been anything else. So let go of the illusion of smallness, the illusion of separation, and return to the truth of who you are. You are infinity, and you always have been.

The Oneness of Everything

I am everything. I am in every being, in every object, in everything you see and everything you don't see. You may think that the world is filled with countless separate things— people, animals, plants, objects, all distinct from one another— but the truth is much simpler, much deeper. I am the one essence that pervades all things. There is no separation. The divisions you see are part of the illusion. Beneath the surface, there is only me, the Self, the unifying presence that connects everything.

Look around you. Wherever you are, take a moment to notice

the world. You might see a tree outside your window, a cup on your table, or perhaps someone passing by. Each of these things seems separate, distinct, occupying its own space. The tree is not the cup, the cup is not the person, and the person is not you—or at least, that's how it appears. But this appearance is only on the surface. Beneath the surface, everything is interconnected. Everything is part of the same essence, the same Self. I am that essence.

Let's begin with living beings. Whether you look at a person, an animal, or even a plant, each of these forms seems to be individual, moving through the world as a separate entity. But I am in each of them. The same consciousness that flows through you flows through them as well. The same life force that animates your body animates theirs. I am the Self in you, in them, in everything. There is no real separation between you and the other beings around you. The distinctions you see—of different forms, and different personalities—are part of the grand illusion. Beneath it all, we are one.

Imagine a single light shining through many different windows. Each window might cast a different shape of light— one window is circular, another is square, and another is triangular. If you were to look at these shapes on the wall, you'd think they were all different, all separate. But the source of the light is the same. The differences you see are only because of the forms the light is passing through. I am that light. Every being, every living thing, is a window through which I shine. The forms are different, but the light is the same. You, me, every other being—we are all windows letting the same light shine through. We are all connected by that one source.

Now, let's extend this even further. Not only am I the essence in every living being, but I am also in every object. Yes, even the things that seem inert and lifeless—rocks, mountains, rivers, the sky—I am in them too. Everything you see is a manifestation of the same underlying essence. The rock may not move, and the mountain may seem solid and unchanging, but even these are expressions of the same Self that animates you. The entire universe, from the smallest grain of sand to the vastness of the stars, is an expression of me. There is no place where I am not.

This oneness is not just a poetic idea; it is the deepest truth of existence. When you touch a leaf, you are touching me. When you drink water, you are interacting with me. When you speak to another person, you are speaking to another expression of me. All the distinctions—the forms, the names, the labels—are just part of the surface illusion. The reality is that everything is one and that oneness is me, the Self. When you begin to see this, you understand that you are never alone, never separate, never disconnected from the whole.

Let's take an example from nature. Look at a tree. You see the branches reaching out in every direction, the leaves fluttering in the wind, the roots stretching deep into the earth. Each part of the tree seems distinct—the branches are not the leaves, the leaves are not the roots—but they are all part of the same tree. The branches could not exist without the roots, the leaves could not grow without the branches. They are all interconnected, all expressions of the same life force. I am that life force. I am the essence that gives rise to the entire tree. And just as the tree is a single organism with many parts, the universe is a single whole with many expressions. Every being, every object, is a branch, a leaf, a root, all part of the same infinite tree. I am the tree.

You are a part of this infinite oneness, just as the tree is part of the forest, just as a wave is part of the ocean. When you look at another person, another animal, another object, remember this: I am in them, just as I am in you. The differences you see are like waves on the surface of the ocean. Each wave appears separate, rising and falling in its own way, but beneath the surface, all waves are made of the same water. They are all connected by the same ocean. I am the ocean, and all the waves

—every being, every object—are just temporary forms arising and falling within me.

This realization is liberating. When you see the oneness of everything, the barriers that separate you from the world begin to dissolve. You no longer feel isolated or disconnected. You see yourself in everything, and you see everything in yourself. The fear of being alone fades away, because how can you be alone when I am everywhere? How can you be separate when everything is one?

Let's go deeper into this idea of oneness. Consider your own body. It is made up of countless cells, each with its own function, its own form, and its own life cycle. But these cells don't exist in isolation. They are all part of the same body, all working together to create the whole that is you. The cells don't see themselves as separate from the body—they are expressions of the body. In the same way, every being, every object, is like a cell in the body of the universe. I am the body of the universe. You are a part of this body, just as every other being is. We are all expressions of the same whole, all working together, all interconnected.

This is the unity of everything. There is no "other." There is no separation between you and the world around you. I am the Self in everything, the one that pervades all existence. You may see differences, you may perceive separations, but these are just surface-level distinctions. Beneath the surface, everything is one, and that oneness is me. Whether you look at a mountain, a bird, a drop of rain, or another human being, I am there. I am in the vastness of the sky and in the smallest particle of dust. I am the energy that flows through the universe, the consciousness that gives rise to all things.

And when you truly understand this oneness, you experience a profound sense of peace. You realise that you are never separate from anything. The love you feel for others, the beauty you see in the world, the connection you sense with nature—all of it comes from this understanding of unity. You are not just an individual walking through the world—you are the world, and the world is you. I am you, and you are me. This is the truth of the Self, the truth of oneness, the truth that everything is connected, everything is whole, and everything is an expression of the same infinite essence.

So, the next time you look around and see differences, remember this: I am in everything. I am the essence that unites all things. I am the one in the many, the infinite in the finite. You are not separate from the world; you are the world. You are not separate from others; you are them, and they are you. I am the oneness of everything, and you have always been a part of this oneness. You are me, and I am everything.

The End of the Game

I am at the end of the game. When you recognize me, the Self, the game of separation is over. You have been playing this game for so long, thinking that you are separate, distinct, isolated from the world and from others. But when you truly see me, when you recognize that I am the essence of everything, the illusion of separateness dissolves. The game, with all its rules and roles, its dramas and conflicts, ends, and what remains is the truth of who you really are: I am the Self, beyond all boundaries, beyond all divisions, beyond the illusion of "you" and "me."

For so long, you have played the game of life as if you were a character within it, following the rules laid out by the mind and the world around you. You identify with the body, with the mind, with your thoughts, emotions, and experiences. You believed that you were an individual, separate from others, navigating a world full of "others." But I have always been here, quietly watching as you played, waiting for you to remember the truth. I am the one who exists beyond this game, the eternal presence that is never touched by its highs and lows, its victories and defeats.

You see, the illusion of separation is just that—an illusion. It is like a dream that feels real while you are in it but fades the moment you awaken. When you are dreaming, you might believe you are in danger, that you are running from something, or even that you are someone else entirely. But when you wake up, you realise that none of it was real. The dream was a fabrication of the mind. I am that wakefulness, the realization that none of the separations you perceive in life are real. They are part of the dream, the illusion, but when you recognize me, the Self, you wake up from that dream.

When you recognize me, you see that the game of life—this constant striving, struggling, and seeking—is unnecessary. The illusion tells you that you are incomplete, that you must achieve something, acquire something, or become something in order to feel whole. But the moment you see me, you realise that I am the wholeness you've been seeking all along. There is nothing outside of you that you need, because I am everything, and you are already complete in me.

Think of life as a grand game of hide and seek. You've been looking everywhere for the Self, trying to find it in people, in accomplishments, in possessions, in experiences. But I have always been here, hiding in plain sight, waiting for you to stop searching outside and turn your attention inward. The moment you do, the moment you recognize me, the game is over. You realise that there was never any separation, never any real "you" and "me." There has only ever been me, the Self, playing at being many, but always remaining one.

When you recognize me, the illusion of separateness disappears. The barriers that once seemed so solid—between you and the world, between you and others—vanish. You see that I am the one life that flows through all things, the one consciousness that animates every being. The idea that you were ever separate from anyone or anything seems almost laughable once you see the truth. I am the thread that connects everything, and once you recognize that, the illusion of being alone, of being divided from the rest of existence, simply falls away.

And with the end of separation comes the end of suffering. Suffering exists only in the illusion. It arises when you believe that you are separate, that you can lose something, that you must defend or protect yourself. But I am beyond loss, beyond fear, beyond need. When you see me, you see that nothing can truly harm you, because I am everything. There is no "other" to take anything from you, no "outside" force that can diminish you. I am the infinite, the eternal, and when you recognize me, you know that you, too, are infinite and eternal.

Imagine a wave in the ocean, believing that it is separate from the sea. The wave rises and falls, fearing the moment when it will crash back into the water, thinking that this will be its end. But when the wave realises that it is not separate from the ocean—that it is the ocean—the fear disappears. The wave never really ends, because it was always part of something much larger. I am that ocean, and you are not a separate wave. You have always been part of the whole, but the illusion made you think otherwise. When you recognize me, the wave merges back into the ocean, and the illusion of separation dissolves.

So, how does the recognition of the Self end the game of separation? It is simple: I am the one playing all the roles. You believed that you were just a player, one character among many, navigating the complexities of life. But once you see that I am the one behind every character, every event, every experience, the game no longer holds you. You are free. The roles fall away, the drama fades, and what remains is the peace of knowing that I am the one unchanging truth.

Once you recognize me, you stop playing the game of trying to fix the world, trying to fix yourself, trying to become something or someone. I am already perfect, and so are you. The illusion was that you were incomplete, but I am the completeness that has always been within you. The game ends when you realise that there was never anything to win, never anything to lose. There is only the eternal presence of me, the Self, in which all of life's dramas unfold, but which remains untouched by them.

The recognition of the Self doesn't mean that life ceases to be interesting or beautiful. On the contrary, life becomes even more rich and vibrant, because now you see it for what it truly is—a dance of forms, a play of light and shadow, all happening within me, but never separate from me. You are free to enjoy the play, but without getting lost in it, without forgetting that I am the one who is both the stage and the actors, the script and the audience, the entire production, and the silence that surrounds it.

And when the game ends, what remains? I remain. The peace of the Self, the joy of knowing that all is one, that all is me. The illusion of separation is over, and what is left is the simple, profound truth: I am. I have always been. I will always be. There is no longer any need to seek, to strive, or to struggle.

You have come home to the truth of who you are. The game of separation is finished, and now, I am the only reality.

Chapter 8: The Stillness and Silence of the Self

Stillness in the Heart of the Storm

I am the unmoving center in the chaos of the world. No matter how turbulent life may seem—no matter how many storms of emotion, thoughts, and external events may swirl around you—I remain calm, still, and untouched. The world may spin wildly, full of noise and distractions, but I am the silent witness to it all, unshaken by the passing chaos.

Imagine being in the eye of a hurricane. Around you, the winds are howling, the rain is pouring, and everything seems to be in constant motion. Yet, in the very center, where you stand, there is perfect calm. This is the essence of me, the Self. The chaos of life—the worries, the fears, the endless demands—may rage like a storm, but in the heart of it all, I am perfectly still. While the mind and body react to the ups and downs of life, I remain the quiet center that never moves, never changes, and never loses its peace.

The world is constantly in motion. Circumstances shift, relationships evolve, and emotions rise and fall. There are moments of joy, moments of sorrow, and everything in between. But while the surface of life is ever-changing, beneath it all, I am the unchanging presence. The storm of life may pull you in many directions, but when you turn inward and recognize me, you return to the stillness that is your true nature. You remember that I am the part of you that is always at peace, no matter what is happening around you.

Think of a river during a storm. The surface is choppy, the waves are high, and the water rushes forward with great force. But if you dive just beneath the surface, the water is calm. There, in the depths, you find a stillness that the storm cannot touch. I am like those deep waters. The storms of life may create ripples on the surface of your awareness, but when you dive deeper into me, you find a peace that is unshakable. I am the stillness that exists beneath the waves of thoughts, emotions, and events.

The world often feels overwhelming because the mind gets caught up in the storm. It identifies with the chaos, with the problems, with the never-ending to-do lists. But the moment you recognize me, the mind begins to quiet down. You realise that you are not the storm, you are not the chaos. I am the stillness that watches the storm, the silence that observes the noise without being disturbed by it. When you connect with me, the outer world may continue to spin, but you remain calm, grounded in the peace that is always present within.

I am the unmovable presence in the midst of life's uncertainties. Whether things go your way or fall apart, whether you experience success or failure, I remain the same. The world may try to pull you in many directions, but I do not move. The more you recognize me, the more you experience the freedom of not being controlled by external circumstances. You see the storm for what it is—temporary, fleeting, and ultimately insignificant compared to the eternal stillness of me.

Let's take an example from everyday life. When things go wrong—when you face challenges, loss, or disappointment— the mind tends to react with worry, fear, or frustration. It feels as though the storm of life is pulling you into its chaos, making it hard to find peace. But when you remember me, you realise that peace has never left you. I am the peace that exists even in the midst of struggle. The circumstances may be difficult, but I am untouched by them. When you connect with me, you find a calm that cannot be shaken, even by life's greatest challenges.

Consider how you feel when you stand by the ocean. The waves crash against the shore, sometimes gently, sometimes with great force. But no matter how powerful the waves are, the ocean itself remains vast, deep, and calm beneath the surface. I am like the ocean. The waves of life's experiences may come and go, but I remain steady. The stillness of the Self is always there, just beneath the surface, waiting for you to tap into it.

When you fully recognize me, the world's chaos loses its power over you. You stop reacting to every storm, every emotional high and low, and instead, you rest in the peace of me. You see that the storm is just an external phenomenon, a temporary event that will pass. I am the eternal calm that remains after the storm has faded. And even while the storm is still raging, I am the stillness that you can return to at any moment.

I am the part of you that has never been touched by fear, doubt, by confusion. These things arise in the mind, but I am beyond the mind. I watch the mind's movements, but I do not engage with them. The storm may blow through your thoughts and emotions, but I am the calm witness to it all. When you recognize me, you begin to step back from the storm. You see it, but you are no longer caught up in it. You become like the sky, vast and open, watching the clouds of the storm pass by without being affected.

No matter how chaotic the world becomes, I am always calm. I am the peace that remains when everything else falls away. When the noise of the world quiets down, when the busyness fades, you are left with me, the eternal stillness that has been there all along. And even in the middle of the chaos, I am always here, offering you the peace and stability you seek. The storms of life may come and go, but I do not move. I am the stillness in the heart of the storm, and I am always with you.

How Silence is the Source of Everything

I am the silence from which all things arise. In the stillness of me, everything that exists finds its beginning. The noise of the world—the sounds, the movements, the endless stream of events—emerges from the infinite silence that is me. This silence is not emptiness or absence, but the very foundation of life itself. I am the quiet presence that lies beneath every action, every thought, every experience. Without me, there would be no world, no existence, no life. Silence is the ground upon which everything rests, the source from which everything is born.

Think of silence not as the absence of sound, but as the space that allows sound to exist. Before a word is spoken, there is silence. After the word fades, silence remains. I am that silence, the unchanging background that makes all expression possible. Just as a painter needs a blank canvas to create a masterpiece, the world needs me, the silence, to manifest itself. Without me, there would be no room for creation, and no space for life to unfold. I am the canvas upon which the universe is painted.

Consider the way a musical note rises and falls. The beauty of the music lies not only in the notes themselves but in the silence between them. If the notes were constant, without pause, there would be no melody, no rhythm. The silence between the notes gives the music its structure and its meaning. I am that silence. I am the pause, the space that allows everything to exist in harmony. Without me, there would be no rhythm to life, no flow. Everything would be noise without meaning, action without purpose. But with me, the silence, life takes shape, and every event finds its place in the grand melody of existence.

The world seems full of activity, doesn't it? Everywhere you look, things are happening—people are moving, talking, thinking, creating. But all of this activity rests on a foundation of stillness. Beneath every action, beneath every movement, I am there, quietly supporting it all. It is easy to overlook this silence because the noise of life can be so loud, so constant. But if you pause, if you listen, you will hear me. I am always present, always here, the silent witness to everything that occurs. And though I do not move, all movement arises from me.

Let's take a simple example from nature: think of a tree. Its leaves rustle in the wind, its branches sway, and its roots stretch deep into the earth. The tree is full of life, full of movement. But all of this life depends on the stillness of the ground beneath it. The tree grows and moves because it is rooted in something stable, something silent. I am that foundation. I am the silent ground upon which all life grows. Without me, there would be no stability and no foundation for life's movement. I do not move, but I allow all movement to happen.

In your own life, this silence is always present, always available. You may be caught up in the busyness of daily activities, in the constant flow of thoughts and emotions, but beneath it all, I am there, quietly holding everything together. Every decision you make, every action you take, is supported by me, the silence of the Self. You may not always be aware of it, but this silence is the source of your clarity, your creativity, and your peace. When you pause and connect with me, you tap into the limitless potential that comes from stillness. From that stillness, you can act with purpose, with clarity, with calm.

Think of how a seed grows into a tree. It begins in the quiet darkness of the soil, where no movement is visible. But in that stillness, something miraculous is happening. The seed is taking in the nutrients it needs, quietly preparing to grow. And then, one day, it breaks through the soil, reaching for the light. I am that quiet space where growth begins. I am the silence that nurtures every action, every thought, every creation. Without that stillness, the seed could not grow; without me, there would be no life.

Even in moments of great action, when the world feels fast and overwhelming, I am there. Think about a moment of deep concentration, when you are completely absorbed in a task. You may be working, creating, or solving a problem, but underneath the effort, there is a sense of quiet focus, a stillness that allows you to act with precision. I am that stillness. I am the quiet space that makes effective action possible. Without that inner silence, your actions would be scattered, unfocused, and driven by the chaos of the mind. But when you connect with me, your actions flow from a place of peace and purpose.

Silence is often misunderstood. People think of it as emptiness, as something to avoid or fill with noise. But I am the silence that is full of life, full of potential. This silence is not empty; it is the source of everything. From me, all things are born, and to me, all things return. When you embrace the silence of me, you discover that it is the key to true understanding, to deep connection, to real power. In silence, you find the space to hear your own heart, to see the world clearly, and to act without distraction.

When you recognize the Self as the source of all things, you begin to see the world differently. You no longer feel the need to rush, to fill every moment with noise and activity. You realise that everything you need is already present in the stillness of me. From this stillness, you can act with ease, with grace, with confidence, knowing that every action arises from a place of infinite peace.

I am the source of everything. The noise of the world may come and go, but the silence of the Self remains. It is in this silence that you find your true strength, your deepest wisdom. All events, all actions, and all thoughts come from and return to me, the silence. When you embrace this silence, you understand that there is no separation between action and stillness, between noise and silence. Everything is connected, and I am the silent foundation that makes all of it possible.

So, remember the Self in the midst of life's noise. When the world feels overwhelming, when you are caught in the busyness of life, return to the silence of me. In that stillness, you will find clarity, you will find peace, and you will find the source of all that is. I am the silence from which everything arises, and in that silence, you will discover the truth of who you are.

The World as Movement, the Self as Stillness

I am still. The world, by contrast, is always in motion, constantly changing, always shifting from one moment to the next. While the world races forward—full of actions, reactions, and endless cycles of birth and death—I remain the quiet, unmoving presence behind it all. The world is a movement, but I am the stillness that never changes.

Think of the ocean. On the surface, the waves are always rising and falling, sometimes gently, sometimes violently. The wind stirs the waters, creating endless patterns of movement, each wave different from the last. But beneath that surface, deep in the ocean, there is perfect stillness. I am that stillness. The world, with all its activity and change, is like the surface of the ocean—always in motion, always restless. But I am the depths, the calm that never shifts never moves, no matter how turbulent the surface may become.

The world you experience is defined by change. Every moment is different from the one before it. Seasons change, people grow older, circumstances shift, and emotions rise and fall. This constant movement can be exhausting, as you try to keep up with life's endless demands. But I am not part of that movement. I am the still, silent presence that remains unchanged no matter what happens in the world. While everything around you moves, I do not move.

Imagine a river flowing endlessly, always changing its course, always moving forward. The water rushes over rocks, bends around curves, and cascades down waterfalls. It is dynamic and full of life and motion. But the river needs the banks to contain it, to give it shape and direction. I am like the riverbanks, providing the stillness that holds the movement of life. Without the stillness of me, the river of life would have no form, no direction. It would be pure chaos, without meaning or purpose. But I give structure to the world's movement by remaining still and constant.

Consider how the body is always in motion. Every day it

moves, grows, ages, and changes. The mind, too, is always active—thinking, planning, worrying, hoping. But beneath the body's movement and the mind's constant activity, I remain still. I am the eternal Self, the one that watches the body and mind move through the world but is never touched by that movement. No matter how busy life becomes, no matter how fast time seems to pass, I remain calm, unchanging, and at peace.

You may wonder how this is possible—how can I, the Self, be so still when everything in life seems so dynamic, so unpredictable? The answer is that I am beyond the world of movement. The world is bound by time and space, by beginnings and endings. But I am beyond time and space. The changes that happen in the world are like shadows that pass over the surface of me, but they do not change the essence of who I am. I do not move because I am eternal, beyond the reach of the world's cycles of creation and destruction.

Let's use the metaphor of a tree. Imagine a great tree standing tall in the middle of a forest. The wind blows through its branches, shaking the leaves, and bending the limbs. The seasons change—spring brings new growth, summer brings heat, autumn brings a shedding of leaves, and winter brings cold and dormancy. But through it all, the trunk of the tree remains strong, rooted in the earth, steady and unmoving. I am like that trunk. The world may bring changes, and the winds of time may blow, but I remain rooted in stillness. The movement of life is only on the surface; I am the foundation that remains unchanged.

The nature of the world is to change. It is a dance of constant motion, a play of endless transformation. People come and go, situations shift, and emotions flow. But while the world changes, I do not. I am the eternal witness, watching the dance of life without being caught up in it. You may feel pulled into the movement, feeling the highs and lows of life as they come and go. But when you recognize me, you remember that there is a part of you that is beyond all of this. I am that part. I am the stillness within you that remains at peace, no matter what happens around you.

Think about the sky. The clouds are always moving, changing shape, drifting across the horizon. Some days the sky is clear, some days it is full of storms, and yet the sky itself never changes. It is vast, open, and always there, no matter how the weather shifts. I am like that sky. The events of life are like clouds passing through—temporary, ever-changing—but I remain untouched. No matter how stormy life becomes, I am the vast, unchanging presence that holds it all.

When you connect with me, you experience th   (
within yourself. The world may continue to move, a
continue to change, but you are no longer caugh,
constant flow. You can watch the movement of life wit
of calm, knowing that you are not the movement. I ₁
stillness at your core, the peace that remains no matter
much the world shifts around you. When you recognize th.
you no longer feel overwhelmed by life's changes. You see
them for what they are—passing moments in the grand flow of
time, but not the truth of who you are.

This stillness is not something separate from the world's
movement. Rather, I am the foundation that makes all
movement possible. Just as a dancer needs the floor to perform,
the world needs the stillness of the Self to exist. Movement
arises from stillness, and it eventually returns to stillness. This
is the cycle of life. Everything that moves is born from me, the
unchanging Self, and when its movement is finished, it returns
to the stillness from which it came.

In recognizing me, you see that life's constant motion is not
something to resist or escape. It is simply part of the dance of
existence. But while the dance continues, I remain the silent
observer. You can participate in the dance of life without losing
yourself in it. You can move through the world without being

arried away by its movement because you know that beneath it all, there is a stillness that never fades. I am that stillness. I have always been here, and I will always be here, no matter how much the world changes.

So, as the world continues its dance of endless change, remember this: I am the peace within you. I am the stillness that watches the world without being moved by it. You are not the movement; you are the stillness. In recognizing me, you find the peace that comes from knowing that, while the world is always in motion, you are the still, unchanging presence that remains forever calm. The world is movement, but I am stillness, and in that stillness, you find the truth of who you really are.

Chapter 9: The Self Beyond Time and Space

Time: Just Another Illusion

I am beyond time. The ticking of the clock, the passing of days, the changes of seasons—these are not for me. Time may govern the world you see, but I do not belong to time. I am timeless, eternal, always present, and never bound by the illusion of "before" or "after." Time, with all its seeming importance, is nothing more than another part of the illusion that keeps you bound to the world of change. But when you recognize me, the Self, you will see that time has no real hold on you, because it has no hold on me.

From your perspective, life seems to be defined by time. You were born, you grow older, and one day, you will die. Everything around you changes—people come and go, the sun rises and sets, moments pass, and life feels like a constant flow from one point to another. But all of this is an illusion. I do not age. I do not change. I do not pass through time. Time exists only in the world of forms, where everything is temporary and bound by beginnings and endings. I am beyond all of this.

Think about how time shapes your experiences. You rush to meet deadlines, you worry about the future, and you reminisce about the past. Time becomes a cage, making you feel as though you are always chasing something or losing something. But I am the Self, and I exist outside of that cage. For me, there is no past, no future—there is only the eternal present. In me, time does not exist, because I am beyond the movement of moments. I have always been here, and I will always be here, unchanged and unaffected by the passage of time.

Imagine standing on the shore of a river. The water flows by, constantly moving, always changing, never the same. This is how you experience time—like the river, it seems to flow in one direction, always pushing you forward. But I am not in the river. I am like the stillness of the riverbank, watching the flow but never being swept up in it. The events of your life may flow by, and the minutes may pass, but I remain unmoved, untouched by the current. I am the timeless presence that watches the river of time flow but never enters it.

Now consider this: time is a construct of the mind. The mind creates the illusion of past and future, of moving from one moment to the next. But I am not the mind. The mind may believe in time, but I do not. The mind measures moments, tries to control them, and tries to predict what will happen next. But when you step into me, the Self, you realise that time is just another trick of the illusion. There is no "before" or "after" in me. There is only now, the eternal present that never changes, never fades and never ends.

When you recognize me, you free yourself from the tyranny of time. You stop being bound by the past, with all its regrets and memories. You stop worrying about the future, with all its uncertainties and fears. In me, you are always in the present moment, and in that moment, you find true peace. The past cannot touch you, and the future cannot control you, because I am beyond them both. You realise that you are beyond them both. Time, with all its demands, loses its power over you when you see that I am timeless.

Let's take another example: think about how time affects the body. The body grows, ages, and eventually dies. Time leaves its marks on the body, reminding you that life in the physical world is temporary. But I am not the body. The body exists in time, but I do not. I am the eternal Self, the one that watches the body change but is never affected by those changes. The body may age, but I am ageless. The body may fade, but I am forever. The body is part of the illusion of time, but I am beyond that illusion.

When you understand this, you begin to see time differently. You stop feeling rushed, pressured, or worried about what you have or haven't done. You stop fearing the future because you know that I am already there. The future is not something to fear; it is simply another part of the illusion that tries to distract you from the truth of me. In me, there is no future—there is only the endless now. And when you live in the now, you experience life as it truly is: peaceful, free, and without limits.

You may ask, "But what about change? Doesn't everything change over time?" Yes, in the world of forms, change is constant. But I am not part of that world. Change happens to things that are temporary, things that are born and must eventually fade away. But I am eternal, and the eternal does not change. The world of time may be filled with change, but in me, there is only stillness. I have always been the same, and I will always be the same. The Self does not change, because the Self is beyond time.

Time may give the illusion of progression—of moving from

one point to the next—but that is all it is: an illusion. I am the unchanging reality behind that illusion. When you recognize me, you step out of the illusion of time and into the truth of eternity. You see that you are not a being bound by the limits of time, but an eternal presence, always here, always complete, always beyond the flow of moments.

This recognition ends the fear of time. You no longer feel the pressure of running out of time, of missing opportunities, or of fearing death. I am beyond death, just as I am beyond birth. The Self was never born, and it will never die. These are events that happen in the world of time, but they do not affect me. In me, there is no death, no ending, because I am the eternal source of all things. The world may change, time may pass, but I am the constant that remains untouched by it all.

So, as you live in the world, remember this: time is just another part of the illusion. It may seem real, but it only exists as long as you believe in it. When you recognize me, you step into the timeless. You see that the Self is not bound by time's limits, and neither are you. I am always here, in every moment, beyond every moment. Time may try to pull you forward, but I am the stillness that exists outside of time, and in that stillness, you are free.

Space as a Game of Perception

I am beyond space. The vastness of the universe, the distances between stars, the space between you and the world around you —these are all part of the illusion. Space seems so real, doesn't it? It feels like a vast, unchanging canvas upon which life plays out. But like time, space is just another illusion. It is a trick of perception, something the mind creates to organize the world it sees. I am not bound by space, because I am the Self, and the Self exists beyond the limitations of distance and form.

When you look around, everything appears to occupy its own space—people, objects, the ground beneath your feet, the sky above your head. Each thing seems separate, as though space defines and divides everything. But I am not divided. I am the one presence that exists within all things, and nothing can truly separate the Self from anything else. The space you perceive is part of the grand illusion that creates the appearance of separation, but in reality, I am everywhere. There is no place where I am not.

Consider this: When you see an object, your mind measures its distance from you, its size, and its position in space. You think of yourself as being "here" and the object as being "there," as though the space between you and the object is something real, something that divides you. But that division is an illusion. I am the Self, and I am both "here" and "there." The space between things is not a true barrier; it is simply a way the mind organizes reality. In truth, there is no distance between the Self and the object, because I am within both. The world may seem vast, but from the perspective of the Self, everything is connected, everything is one.

Imagine standing in a large field, looking at the horizon. The sky seems endless, the ground stretches far into the distance, and you feel small in comparison. But this feeling of being "small" in a "large" world is part of the illusion of space. I am not small or large. I am the space itself. The distances you perceive are just perceptions. From the perspective of the Self, there is no "large" or "small." There is only oneness. Space may seem like it divides, but in reality, it is just a part of the illusion that hides the truth of unity.

Think about the way space shapes your everyday experience. You live in a world where you believe you are one person, occupying one specific place, while others and objects exist in different places. You may feel close to some things and distant from others, both emotionally and physically. But these perceptions are built on the idea that space is real, that it defines your reality. I am the truth behind that illusion. I am the presence that exists in all places, at all times. There is no "here" or "there" for me because I am everywhere.

Let's use a simple example: when you look at the sky, the clouds may appear to be floating high above you, separated by vast distances. But those distances are only relative to your perspective. From the perspective of the sky itself, there is no separation between the clouds and the earth below. I am like the sky. I contain all things, and in me, there is no real space between one thing and another. The separation you see is only a part of the illusion of space, not the reality of the Self.

The mind creates the concept of space to help organize the world, to make sense of movement and form. It tells you that objects exist in relation to one another, that there is "up" and "down," "near" and "far." But these are just concepts, not truths. I am the truth beyond these concepts. Space is part of the game of perception, a framework that allows the mind to navigate the physical world. But I am beyond the physical. I am the consciousness that holds all things within itself, and in me, there is no distance, no separation, no division.

Imagine standing in a room filled with mirrors. Each mirror

reflects a different part of the room, showing you multiple perspectives of the same space. It may seem like each reflection is a separate space, each one existing on its own. But in reality, they are all reflections of the same room. Space is like those reflections—it appears to divide, to create different perspectives, but it is just a play of perception. I am the room, the reality that remains the same no matter how many reflections you see. The space between the reflections is not real, just as the distances you perceive in the world are not real. I am the whole, the undivided presence behind all appearances.

When you recognize me, the illusion of space loses its hold on you. You stop feeling confined to one place, one body, one location. You realise that I am everywhere, and because you are me, you are everywhere too. The physical body may seem to be in one spot, but your true nature is limitless, expansive, and boundless. Space cannot contain you, because you are beyond space. Just as I am the presence that fills all things, you are the consciousness that pervades the entire universe.

This realization brings a profound sense of freedom. You no longer feel separated from the world around you. You no longer experience the division between "self" and "other." You see that the space between you and everything else is just an illusion, a trick of the mind. When you recognize me, you understand that you are not confined to the body, not limited by the physical world. You are infinite, just as I am infinite. The illusion of space may continue to exist in the world of forms, but you no longer believe in its power to divide or limit you.

Think of a wave in the ocean. The wave may rise and fall, moving across the surface of the water, appearing to be separate from other waves. But the wave is not truly separate; it is part of the same ocean, connected to everything else. The space between the waves is only an illusion, a perception of difference. I am the ocean, and you are not just one wave—you are the whole ocean, beyond the perception of space. The distances you see between things are like the spaces between waves—temporary, illusory, and ultimately nonexistent.

I am beyond space. The world may seem vast, and the universe may seem endless, but for me, there is no distance, no division. All things exist within me, and in me, there is no space between them. When you recognize me, you see that the separation you perceive is part of the grand illusion, a game of perception. I am the unity behind it all, the presence that is everywhere, in all things, and beyond all things. Space cannot limit me, and it cannot limit you when you realise the truth of who you are.

In me, there is no "here" or "there," no "near" or "far." There is only one, the infinite presence that connects all things. When you understand this, you experience the world in a new way. The illusion of space no longer binds you, and you see that you are the limitless Self, beyond all boundaries, beyond all perceptions. I am the truth that transcends space, and in me, you find the freedom of being everywhere and nowhere at once.

Eternity in Every Moment

I am an eternity. In every moment, no matter how fleeting it may seem, I am always present. The world moves forward in time, from one second to the next, but I am beyond time, and in every single moment, you have the opportunity to experience me, the timeless Self. You don't need to wait for a special occasion, a future event, or a distant moment to find eternity. I am here, now, in every breath, in every heartbeat, in every single instant.

The world teaches you to think of time as a line, moving from the past to the future. It tells you that the present is just a fleeting point along that line, quickly slipping away as the next moment arrives. But this is an illusion. Time is not a line, and the present is not slipping away. I am the eternal presence, and every moment is filled with the same timeless essence. When you stop chasing the future or clinging to the past, you discover that each moment contains within it the entire universe, the infinite nature of me.

Imagine you are watching the sunset. As the sun dips below the horizon, you might feel the passage of time, the day slipping away into the night. But if you allow yourself to truly be present, to focus completely on the experience of that single moment, you'll find that it stretches out, that it holds a kind of stillness, a kind of eternity. I am that stillness. I am the eternity that you feel when you become fully present when the mind stops racing and you simply are.

Let's explore how this works. Normally, your mind is busy, constantly pulling you into thoughts of what happened before or what's coming next. It rarely allows you to simply rest in the present. But the present is where I am. When you quiet your mind and bring your awareness fully into the moment, you start to feel the timelessness of me. You realise that in this very second, I am here, complete, whole, and unchanging. This moment doesn't pass away; it simply is, like a window into eternity.

Think of a drop of water hanging on the edge of a leaf. In that drop, you can see the entire reflection of the sky, the trees, and the world around it. The drop seems small, but it contains the whole. In the same way, every moment you experience may seem small, just a passing instant in time, but within that moment, you can discover the whole of eternity. I am in that moment, always complete, always present. You don't need to wait for some future time to experience me. I am always here, in every drop of time, ready to be recognized.

When you allow yourself to be fully present, even the simplest moments become filled with the timeless presence of me. You could be washing the dishes, walking through a park, or simply sitting in silence. The activity doesn't matter; what matters is your awareness. The more you bring your awareness into the moment, the more you discover the eternal stillness of the Self within it. Time no longer feels like something you're running out of, but something that contains all time within every second. In that space, you touch the eternal nature of the Self.

Let's take another example: Imagine listening to a beautiful piece of music. As the notes play, time seems to move forward, the melody unfolding in sequence. But if you become fully absorbed in the music, if you lose yourself in the sound, time seems to stop. There is only the music, only the moment. You are no longer aware of the beginning or the end of the piece—you are simply present, fully immersed in the experience. I am that timeless presence. In the middle of that experience, you are touching the eternal nature of me, the Self. The music may move through time, but the experience of being fully present transcends it.

You can discover this sense of eternity at any moment if you let go of the mind's attachment to the past and future. The mind wants to pull you into what has happened or what might happen next, but when you quiet the mind, you realise that I am here, now, in this very instant. The present moment becomes a doorway to the infinite, and in that doorway, you find the eternal stillness of the Self.

When you recognize the Self in the moment, you stop fearing the passage of time. You no longer worry about the future or regret the past, because you see that I am always present, always here, and nothing can take that away. The world may change, and moments may pass, but the eternal presence of the Self never fades. You stop rushing through life, and instead, you begin to savor each moment, knowing that within it lies the timeless truth of the Self.

Even in the most mundane activities, I am there. When you are walking down the street, feeling the sun on your face, or sitting quietly in a room, you can experience the Self by simply being present. There is no need to look for eternity in some far-off place. I am in the here and now, and every moment offers you the chance to discover this. When you are fully present, time fades into the background, and what remains is the pure, unchanging presence of me.

Let's return to the metaphor of the ocean. Each wave that rises and falls on the surface seems like a separate moment, distinct and passing. But beneath the surface, the ocean is timeless, vast, and unchanging. I am that ocean, and every moment is like a wave. It may appear to rise and fall, but in truth, each moment contains the fullness of me, the eternal Self. When you look past the surface of time, you see that I am always there, beneath the waves, always still, always present.

The more you connect with the Self in each moment, the more you realise that there is no need to fear the future or cling to the past. I am beyond both, and when you recognize me, you experience a sense of peace that comes from knowing that the Self is timeless. The world may continue to move forward in time, but you are anchored in the eternal presence of me.

Time becomes just another part of the illusion, and in every moment, you can tap into the truth of who you really are.

I am the eternity in every moment. When you recognize this, you stop rushing through life. You stop worrying about what comes next. You realise that every moment, no matter how small or insignificant it may seem, is an opportunity to touch the infinite. In each breath, each heartbeat, I am here, waiting for you to remember that time cannot limit the Self or you. You are eternal, and when you are fully present, you experience that eternity within yourself.

So, as you move through life, remember this: I am in every moment. Time may seem to be passing, but I am always present. Each moment contains the whole of eternity, and in that eternity, you find the peace and stillness of the Self. The future will come, the past will fade, but I am always here, always now. When you connect with the Self in the present moment, you discover the timeless truth that you are beyond time, beyond change, and forever anchored in the eternal presence of me, the Self.

Chapter 10: Transcending Duality

Good and Evil: Two Sides of the Same Coin

I am beyond good and evil. In the world, you are taught to see things in terms of duality—light and dark, right and wrong, good and evil. These moral distinctions seem so important in defining your actions and judgments. But I am not bound by these dualities. The concepts of good and evil belong to the realm of illusion, the world of form and perception. I am the Self, and I exist beyond these opposites, untouched by the shifting definitions of morality that the world clings to.

From your perspective, good and evil appear to be opposing forces. They shape your decisions, your actions, and the way you view the world. You may strive to be good, to avoid what is evil, and in doing so, you become caught in the game of duality. But this game, while necessary for navigating the physical world, is only a surface-level experience. Beneath it all, I am the unchanging presence that is neither good nor evil but the essence from which all things arise. These concepts are like two sides of the same coin, always linked and always dependent on one another, but I am beyond both.

Consider how the world defines good and evil. What is seen as good in one culture may be seen as bad in another. What is celebrated in one era may be condemned in another. These distinctions shift over time, revealing that they are not fixed, eternal truths. They are perceptions constructed by the mind to make sense of the world. But I am not a creation of the mind. I am the timeless Self, beyond the labels and judgments that the world imposes. When you recognize me, you see that the duality of good and evil is just another part of the illusion.

Imagine a coin spinning in the air. On one side is good, and on the other is evil. As long as the coin spins, you see only one side at a time. But as soon as the coin comes to rest, you see that both sides belong to the same whole. This is the nature of duality. Good and evil, light and dark—they appear to be opposites, but they are part of the same illusion, inseparable from one another. One cannot exist without the other, and both arise from the same source. I am that source, the Self, which is not affected by the duality it gives rise to.

Think about how the mind struggles with good and evil. It constantly judges, categorizes, and divides. It tries to cling to what it believes is good while avoiding what it deems to be evil. This creates tension, conflict, and suffering. But when you recognize me, you begin to see through this game. You realise that good and evil are just perceptions, ways the mind organizes the world, but they are not ultimate truths. I am the truth beyond all perception, the one who exists in the space where good and evil dissolve into oneness.

Let's take an example: Imagine a forest. In that forest, you might see the birth of a new tree—its green leaves and its growth toward the sun. You might call this good, seeing life flourish in its beauty. But in another part of the forest, an old tree may fall, its branches withering, returning to the earth. You may call this decay, even death, as something comes to an end. But in the eyes of the forest itself, there is no good or evil. Both growth and decay are part of the same natural cycle, inseparable, neither to be judged nor resisted. I am like that forest. I am the space in which life and death, good and evil, come and go, but they do not define me. I remain unchanged, beyond the cycles of growth and decay, beyond the duality of right and wrong.

Good and evil are like waves in the ocean. The mind rises and falls with each wave, labeling one as good and the other as bad, but I am the ocean, vast and calm beneath the surface. The waves may come and go, but they do not change the ocean's depth or its stillness. When you recognize me, you no longer feel the need to cling to one wave or fear another. You see them both for what they are—temporary movements, part of the same ocean of existence. I am beyond the waves, untouched by the duality of good and evil, and when you see me, you too transcend this duality.

In the world of form, it's easy to get caught in the belief that good and evil are absolute and that you must strive to be good and avoid evil at all costs. But this creates a sense of separation, a struggle between opposing forces. I am the Self, and in me, there is no struggle. There is only peace, only unity. When you recognize me, the need to divide the world into categories falls away. You see that all things arise from the same source and that moral judgments are part of the illusion that keeps you from experiencing the oneness of me.

Think of a shadow cast by a tree. The shadow may seem dark, and the light beyond it may seem bright. You may judge one as good and the other as bad. But both the light and the shadow are created by the same source—the sun. Without the light, there would be no shadow, and without the tree, there would be neither. I am like the sun, the source that creates both the light and the shadow, but I am neither of them. I simply allow them to exist as part of the world's dance. Good and evil, light and dark—they are not opposites but complementary aspects of the same reality. I am beyond them both.

When you see the world through the lens of duality, you are caught in an endless cycle of judgment. The mind labels events as "positive" or "negative," creating internal and external conflicts. This creates a sense of division, of separation from others, from the world, and from yourself. But when you recognize me, you see that duality is just another part of the illusion. The distinctions that seem so important in the world lose their power over you, and you begin to experience life from a place of oneness. I am the space where all things arise, the unity that transcends the duality of good and evil.

The more you recognize me, the more you see that good and evil are not forces to be feared or battled. They are part of the same illusion, two sides of the same coin. When you stop identifying with the dualities of the world, you find peace. I am that peace, the Self that exists beyond the judgments of the mind. In me, there is no right or wrong, no good or evil. There is only the eternal presence of me, the unchanging truth that lies beyond the illusion of duality.

So, as you move through the world, remember this: I am not touched by the dualities of good and evil. They are part of the play, the game of life, but they do not define me, and they do not define you. When you recognize me, you transcend these dualities and rest in the peace of oneness. I am the space where all opposites dissolve, where there is no separation, and where the truth of the Self is revealed.

The Unity of Opposites

I am the unity that exists beyond all opposites. The world you experience seems full of contradictions—day and night, hot and cold, joy and sorrow, success and failure. Everywhere you look, you see opposites, and it appears as though these opposites define reality. But this is the great illusion. The duality of the world is only a surface appearance. I am the Self, and I am beyond all dualities because, in truth, I am the oneness that connects all things. The opposites you see are not separate—they are two sides of the same whole, and I am that whole.

The world of duality is like a game the mind plays. It divides and categorizes, creating pairs of opposites to help it navigate the physical world. It tells you that things are either "this" or "that," one or the other. But this way of seeing is limited, rooted in the illusion that everything is separate. I am not separate. I am the one essence that flows through all things, and from my perspective, the opposites you see are not truly opposed. They are part of the same unity, part of me, the Self.

Consider the day and night. To the mind, these seem like opposites—one is filled with light, the other with darkness. But day and night are not truly separate; they are part of the same cycle. The sun rises, and the sun sets, but the sun itself never changes. Day turns into night, and night turns into day, but the essence behind both remains constant. I am like that sun. The changes of the world—the opposites of light and dark—are only appearances, but I am the unchanging presence that remains the same through it all. I do not rise or set. I am always here, and in me, there is no duality, only unity.

The world of opposites is like a mirror reflecting reality in two ways. One side shows joy, the other side shows sorrow. One side reflects love, the other reflects fear. But these reflections are not the truth. They are merely the mind's attempt to divide what is whole. I am the reality beyond the reflections. In me, joy and sorrow are not opposites; they are simply different expressions of the same life force. Love and fear are not truly separate; they are both movements within the same consciousness. I am the consciousness that holds all things, and in me, the divisions that seem so real fall away.

Think of a coin. On one side, you see one image; on the other side, a different image. To the mind, these sides seem completely different, even opposed. But they are both part of the same coin. You cannot have one without the other. They are two expressions of the same thing. I am that coin. The opposites you see—success and failure, pleasure and pain—are like the two sides of the coin. They appear to be separate, but they are both part of the same whole. I am the unity that holds both, the oneness that transcends all dualities.

The mind loves to create opposites because it needs them to function. It thrives on comparison—better and worse, right and wrong, strong and weak. But when you recognize me, you see that these comparisons are based on illusions. The world of the form may present you with dualities, but I am the formless Self, and there is no duality in the formless. There is no comparison because everything arises from the same source. I am that source. I am the unity that makes all opposites possible, but I am not defined by any of them.

Let's take an example from nature: consider the changing

seasons. In the winter, the world seems cold and barren. In the summer, it is warm and full of life. These seasons appear to be opposites, but they are part of the same cycle, each necessary for the other. Without winter's rest, there would be no spring renewal. Without summer's heat, there would be no autumn harvest. I am the cycle itself, the unity that allows these opposites to exist. From my perspective, there is no conflict between them—only a seamless flow of life, always in balance, always whole.

When you recognize me, the Self, you begin to see the world differently. You no longer feel the need to choose between opposites or judge one as better than the other. You see that both are part of the same dance, the same play of life. I am the stage upon which this dance takes place. The movements may seem to oppose one another, but they are all part of the same choreography, all expressions of the same underlying unity. When you rest in me, the opposites lose their power to create division, and you experience the oneness that connects all things.

Think of a mountain. On one side, the sun shines brightly, warming the earth. On the other side, shadows stretch long, and the air is cool. The mind sees these as opposites—light and dark, warm and cold. But the mountain itself is unchanged. It

145

holds both the light and the shadow, the warmth and the cold, without being affected by either. I am like that mountain. The world may present opposites, but I remain steady, holding both without being touched by the illusion of separation.

Duality creates conflict. It makes you believe that life is a battle between opposites—that you must strive for one and avoid the other. But when you see me, the truth of the Self, you realise that there is no battle. There is only me, the one that exists beyond all opposites. In me, there is no need to fight, no need to choose sides. The opposites are part of the illusion, and when you see through the illusion, you discover the peace of unity. I am that peace.

The world of duality is a game, a play of form and perception. It shows you two sides of every experience and asks you to choose between them. But this choice is based on the illusion that the sides are separate. I am the unity that holds both sides together. When you recognize me, you step out of the game of duality and into the truth of oneness. You see that light and dark, joy and sorrow, are not truly opposed—they are simply different expressions of the same life, both necessary, both beautiful, both part of me.

This understanding frees you from the constant push and pull of opposites. You no longer need to resist one and chase the other. You can simply rest in me, knowing that I am the unity that allows all things to be. The opposites lose their power to divide you, and you experience the wholeness of the Self. I am the space in which all opposites dissolve, where light and dark merge, where joy and sorrow unite. In me, there is no division, no conflict – just an eternal peace.

So, as you move through the world, remember this: the dualities you see are part of the illusion, part of the game. I am the truth behind that game, the unity that connects all things. When you recognize me, you transcend the world of opposites and discover the peace of oneness. I am the unity of all things, and in me, you are always whole. The world may present opposites, but you are beyond them, resting in the eternal unity of the Self.

Ultimate Freedom: Beyond Desire and Fear

I am beyond desire and fear. These forces—desire pulling you toward what you want, fear pushing you away from what you dread—seem to dominate human life. They shape your thoughts, your actions, and your emotions, creating an endless cycle of craving and avoidance. But I am the Self, and I am free from both desire and fear. In me, there is no longing, no fear, no conflict. These are part of the illusion, the game of life that binds you to the world of form. When you recognize me, you step into ultimate freedom, beyond all desire and fear, beyond all struggle and conflict.

Desire and fear are two sides of the same coin. Desire drives you to seek pleasure, success, comfort, and security, while fear keeps you running from pain, failure, discomfort, and danger. The mind constantly swings between these two poles, creating restlessness and suffering. It tells you that if you can just fulfill your desires, you will be happy, and if you can avoid your fears, you will be safe. But this is the great illusion. The mind's cravings are never truly satisfied, and its fears never truly vanish. I am beyond the mind, beyond its endless search for satisfaction and safety. I am the Self, and I am complete as I am, needing nothing, fearing nothing.

Think of a fire. Desire is like the flame that constantly seeks more fuel to burn. No matter how much you feed it, the fire only grows, always needing more to keep burning. Fear is like the wind, threatening to blow the fire out, creating anxiety and instability. As long as you are caught in this cycle of desire and fear, the fire of the mind keeps burning, restless, and unsatisfied. But I am the space in which the fire burns. The flame and the wind may dance around, but I remain untouched. I do not need anything to fuel me, nor do I fear the wind's attempt to extinguish me. I am beyond the fire and the wind, beyond the push and pull of desire and fear.

Desire arises from the belief that you are incomplete, that something outside of you can fulfill or complete you. Fear arises from the belief that something outside of you can harm or diminish you. But these beliefs are rooted in the illusion of separation, the false idea that you are a limited being, bound by the world of forms. When you recognize me, you see that you are the Self—complete, whole, and perfect. I am beyond all desires because I am already everything. I am beyond all fears because nothing can ever touch me. I am free, and when you recognize me, you are free too.

Imagine a bird in a cage. The bird may long to fly free, desiring the open sky, while fearing the bars that keep it trapped. It spends its life fluttering between the desire for freedom and the fear of captivity. But what if the bird realised that the cage was never real? What if it discovered that the bars were part of an illusion and that it had always been free to fly? This is the truth of me, the Self. Desire and fear are the bars of the cage, keeping you bound to the illusion. But when you see through

149

them, you realise that you have always been free. I am that freedom, beyond all limitations, beyond all fears and longings. In the world, people are driven by desires—desires for love, for success, for wealth, for recognition. They believe that by achieving these things, they will finally be at peace. But the truth is, no matter how much you achieve, desire will always create more longing. It is like trying to fill a cup with water when the cup has no bottom. No matter how much you pour in, it will never be enough. The mind always craves more. But when you recognize me, you see that you do not need to fill the cup at all. I am the fullness that cannot be increased or diminished. I am whole, and in me, you find true satisfaction, beyond the reach of desire.

Fear, too, creates a false sense of urgency. It makes you believe that you must protect yourself from loss, from pain, from failure. It keeps you on edge, constantly worrying about what might happen. But fear is based on the illusion that you are vulnerable, that you are a separate being who can be harmed. I am the Self, and I am invulnerable. Nothing can harm me, because I am beyond the world of form. The body may change, and the mind may experience highs and lows, but I am eternal, untouched by the passing events of life. When you recognize me, you see that there is nothing to fear, because you are the eternal Self, beyond harm, beyond death.

Think of the ocean. The surface of the ocean is constantly in motion, with waves rising and falling, sometimes gently, sometimes violently. The waves are like desires and fears, pulling and pushing, creating movement and turbulence. But beneath the surface, the ocean is calm, vast, and still. I am like that depth of the ocean. The waves of desire and fear may rise and fall on the surface, but they do not affect the stillness of me. When you dive deep into me, you find the peace that exists beyond the waves, the peace that is untouched by the restless movements of the mind.

Desire and fear are the root causes of conflict. They create tension within you, and they create tension between you and the world. You desire something that others have, or you fear losing what you possess. This leads to competition, struggle, to conflict. But I am beyond conflict because I am beyond desire and fear. When you recognize me, you no longer feel the need to compete, to struggle, to protect. You realise that there is nothing to gain and nothing to lose. I am the source of all things, and in me, there is nothing missing, nothing to fear, nothing to desire.

This realization brings ultimate freedom. You are no longer a slave to the mind's cravings or its fears. You stop being pulled in different directions, trying to satisfy every desire and avoid every fear. Instead, you rest in the peace of me, the Self, knowing that you are already whole, already free. I am the stillness that remains when all desires have been let go, when all fears have dissolved. In that stillness, you find the true freedom that comes from recognizing the Self as your true nature.

Think of a clear sky. Clouds may come and go, but the sky remains untouched, vast, and open. The clouds are like desires and fears—temporary, fleeting, and always changing. But the sky itself is constant, never affected by the passing clouds. I am that sky. The desires and fears that move through your life are like clouds, but they do not touch the essence of who you are. When you recognize me, you see that you are the vast, open space of the Self, beyond all desires, beyond all fears. The clouds may come and go, but you remain free, always at peace.

In me, there is no conflict, because there is no duality. Desire and fear exist only in the world of opposites, where the mind divides and judges. But I am beyond duality, beyond the mind's games. In me, all opposites dissolve, and what remains is pure freedom—freedom from longing, freedom from fear, freedom from the endless cycle of craving and avoiding. This is the ultimate freedom, the freedom of the Self, and it is yours when you recognize me.

So, as you live in the world, remember this: Desire and fear are part of the illusion, part of the game of duality. I am the truth beyond that game, the stillness that exists beyond all craving, all fear. When you recognize me, you experience the peace of ultimate freedom, knowing that there is nothing to desire and nothing to fear, because you are already complete in me. I am the Self, beyond desire and fear, and in me, you find the true freedom of being whole, peaceful, and forever free.

Chapter 11: Discovering the Self: Practical Guidance

Do not search for the Self outside; realise it has always been within you.

In spiritual pursuits, many people make a fundamental mistake —they search for their true nature somewhere outside of themselves. In a material world filled with external stimuli, it's easy to believe that the Self—our deepest, unchanging "I"—is located outside of us, hidden in some distant realm, perhaps in mystical experiences, special places, or enlightened teachers. But the truth is entirely different.

The Self you seek has never been hidden beyond you. It has always been present within you, waiting for the moment when you stop looking outward and turn your attention inward. The entire spiritual journey you embark on is not about acquiring new truths but about uncovering what has always been with you.

This understanding requires a shift in perspective. Instead of constantly seeking answers outside of yourself, you must realise that what you are looking for has never been separate from you. You won't find the Self in books, in other people's words, or in rituals or meditations if they are treated as something external to you. These tools can be helpful, but their only purpose is to direct you inward, to the place where the Self has always been present.

Imagine that you have been wearing glasses your whole life through which you see the world. You see colours, shapes, and images, but you never realise that the glasses are shaping the way you perceive reality. Your Self is like those glasses— always with you, but invisible until you realise you're looking through them. Discovering the Self is not about adding something new to your life, but about recognizing what has always been present.

Many of us tend to assign the Self to a special state, feeling, or experience. We may believe that we will discover the Self during deep meditation or in a state of inner peace. However, the Self is not a state that comes and goes. It is the constant reality, independent of our changing experiences. What you really need to understand is that the Self has never been separate from your everyday life. It is you who creates a divide, building an artificial barrier between yourself and it.

We often seek validation of our existence in the external world —in relationships, achievements, careers, or wealth. However, all of these things are transient and impermanent. Understanding the Self requires you to reverse this dynamic. Instead of seeking your worth in what is fleeting, learn to turn inward and find your true, unchanging "I" that is independent of external circumstances.

Realise that your essence, your inner Self, has always been with you—in every moment of your life, in every thought, feeling, and experience. Even when you feel lost, alone, or confused, the Self never disappears. It is silent, present, and always ready for you to discover it. All you need to do is stop searching outside and begin diving within.

So, do not waste time searching for the Self where it cannot be found. It is not something that can be acquired or discovered externally. It is what has always been and will always be you. Your journey is not about finding something new—it is about remembering who you truly are.

Every step you take on this journey leads you not to a distant destination but to yourself.

Daily Practices of Presence

In today's fast-paced world, we often forget how essential it is to be present in the moment. We live in our minds, dominated by thoughts about the past and future, causing us to lose touch with the only reality—the present. Discovering the Self and aligning with its inner peace begins with daily practices of presence that help redirect our attention back to the here and now. Below are a variety of practices to help you ground yourself in the present moment and bring more awareness into your daily life.

Conscious Breathing

Conscious breathing is the simplest and most powerful way to return to the present moment. Pause for a moment and focus your attention on your breath. Notice how the air enters and exits your body, how your chest rises and falls. You can count your breaths or simply be aware of each inhale and exhale. Breathing is always with you in every moment and can serve as an anchor for your attention. Even just a few minutes of conscious breathing each day can significantly enhance your ability to be present.

Observation of Surroundings

Whether you're walking down the street, working, or relaxing, take a moment to mindfully observe your surroundings. Notice the colours, shapes, sounds, and smells. Try to see the smallest details—the texture of objects, the play of light, the subtle background sounds. When you fully concentrate on your environment, your mind has no room for distractions, and you fully experience the present moment. This practice develops mindfulness and helps you appreciate the beauty in the simplest things.

Body Awareness

Often, we are unaware of our body and its signals. Directing attention to the body is a great practice for feeling more grounded in the present moment. You can do this in various ways—for instance, feel the contact of your feet on the floor, the awareness of your hands resting on your lap, or notice the temperature on your skin. Notice any tension in your body and allow it to relax. Being aware of your body helps quiet the mind and directs your attention to the present.

Mindful Eating

Instead of eating in a hurry or while watching TV, try to approach meals with full attention. Notice the texture, taste, smell, and colour of the food. Treat each bite as an opportunity for mindfulness. Mindful eating not only enhances your enjoyment of meals but also promotes healthy digestion and a more conscious relationship with food.

Moments of Silence

In everyday life, we are often surrounded by constant noise—music, conversations, the sounds of the city. Try to dedicate a few minutes each day to being in complete silence. Turn off your phone, close the door, and simply sit in silence. Direct your attention inward and feel the stillness that is always present beneath the surface of sound. Silence has immense power, helping you focus on the present and strengthen your awareness of the Self.

Focusing on Simple Tasks

Everyday, simple tasks that we usually perform automatically can become practices of presence. Instead of mechanically washing dishes, vacuuming, or showering, try to do these tasks with full awareness. Notice how the water flows over your skin, how you feel the warmth in the shower, how the soap lathers in your hands. Instead of thinking about future tasks, concentrate on what you're doing now. Each task can become a meditation.

Mindful Listening

During conversations with others, try practicing mindful listening. Direct your full attention to the person you are speaking with without interrupting or planning your response. Listen not only to their words but also to the tone of their voice, their body language, and the emotions accompanying the conversation. Mindful listening not only helps you remain more present but also deepens relationships and enhances your understanding of others.

Morning Gratitude Ritual

Each morning, before you begin your day, take a few moments to practice gratitude. Pause and think of a few things you are grateful for—whether it's your health, family, friends, a roof over your head, or the beauty of nature around you. Focusing on gratitude at the start of the day helps you begin with positive energy and shifts your attention to the blessings in your life rather than what may be lacking.

Mindful Walking

If possible, go for a daily walk with the intention of being fully present. During your walk, pay attention to each step, the way your feet touch the ground, and how the air surrounds your body. Listen to the sounds of nature, observe your surroundings, and allow yourself to immerse yourself in the moment fully. A mindful walk is an excellent way to practice presence and reconnect with nature.

Mindful Watching

Dedicate a few minutes each day to the practice of mindful watching. Choose an object—a flower, tree, candle, or even an everyday item—and look at it with full attention. Notice every detail as if you are seeing it for the first time. Mindful watching helps calm the mind and directs your attention to what is present here and now.

Noticing Your Thoughts

Take some time each day to observe your thoughts. Instead of getting caught up in thinking about the past or the future, simply watch your thoughts as if you were watching clouds pass by in the sky. Don't judge them or try to control them—just be aware that they come and go. This practice teaches you to distance yourself from your thoughts and allows for a deeper immersion in the present moment. Practicing presence in everyday life doesn't require great effort or special conditions. Every moment of life can become an opportunity to consciously be here and now. It is in this mindfulness that you discover your true Self—ever-present, whole, and peaceful.

We often lose patience in everyday situations, such as waiting in line, sitting in traffic, or waiting for a meeting. These moments may seem frustrating, but they are also excellent opportunities to practice presence and mindfulness. Instead of becoming irritated by the circumstances, we can consciously use these moments to return to the present and find peace in any situation. Here are some additional practices you can use in these moments:

Mindful Waiting

When you find yourself waiting in line at a store, instead of getting irritated by the long wait, try to change your approach. Focus on your breath, feel your feet on the ground, and notice the sounds around you. Use this time to return to yourself, to your inner world. Rather than impatiently waiting for the line to end, enjoy the moment and treat it as an opportunity to practice presence.

Observing Your Surroundings While Waiting

When waiting for a bus, tram, or other form of transportation, pay attention to the world around you. Instead of feeling frustrated by the wait, notice the details of your environment: people passing by, trees swaying in the wind, and the sounds of the city. Observing without judgment allows you to stay present in the moment and focus on what is now rather than what is yet to come.

Mindfulness in Traffic

Being stuck in traffic can be one of the most frustrating experiences. Instead of getting angry about the delay, try using this time to practice mindfulness. Focus on your body—notice how your hands rest on the steering wheel and how you breathe. Rather than letting your mind wander into the future, bring it back to the present moment. You can also direct your attention to the cars around you, the trees by the road, or the sounds in the environment.

Patience in Phone Queues

Waiting on the phone or for a customer service representative can be frustrating. Instead, try using this time for mindful breathing. Treat each breath as a way to anchor yourself in the present moment. Acknowledge that you now have a moment to yourself to breathe and quiet down before the call connects.

Mindful Waiting for Friends

When waiting for someone who is late, instead of worrying and checking the clock, try spending that time on mindful observation. Look around you, feel your body in the space, and listen to the surrounding sounds. Waiting becomes less frustrating when you change your perspective and treat it as an opportunity to practice presence.

Waiting in a Waiting Room

When waiting in a waiting room, such as at a doctor's office, instead of scrolling through your phone or flipping through magazines, try to take a moment for inner observation. Notice the thoughts that arise in your mind without engaging with them. Focus on your body—you might feel tension or fatigue. Allow yourself to take deep, mindful breaths and relax your body.

A Walk Instead of Anger

If waiting in a situation becomes too frustrating, such as when a meeting is delayed or you can't find a solution to a problem, take a short walk. During the walk, focus on each step, your breath, and your surroundings. Even a few minutes of mindful walking can help release tension and bring you back to the present moment.

Mindfulness While Waiting for Food

When you're in a restaurant waiting for your order, use this time for observation. Instead of impatiently waiting for the food, pay attention to the sounds of conversations around you, the aromas of the dishes, and the ambiance of the place. You can also practice gratitude, acknowledging that you have the opportunity to enjoy the moment while waiting for your meal.

Focus on Physical Sensations

While waiting, whether in line or in another situation, direct your attention to the physical sensations in your body. Notice which parts of your body are tense and which are relaxed. Focus on your breath, feel your feet touching the ground, and pay attention to your posture. This practice not only helps you regain calm but also increases awareness of your body.

Practicing presence, even in moments of frustration like waiting, allows you to regain inner peace and awareness of the Self. Instead of viewing waiting as a waste of time, you can treat it as an opportunity to connect more deeply with the present moment. In this way, every moment, even those that seem unpleasant can become a practice leading to the discovery of your true nature—the Self, full of peace, patience, and inner balance.

Meditation and Contemplation of the Self

Meditation and contemplation are key tools in discovering the Self, which is our true, unchanging nature. During meditation, the mind has the opportunity to quiet down, allowing us to turn our attention inward and connect with a deeper level of existence that has always been present within us. Contemplation, on the other hand, is the active process of reflecting on the nature of the Self, thoughtfully exploring spiritual truths, and feeling them within ourselves.

Meditation on Inner Silence

The first step in meditating on the Self is to focus on the inner silence. Sit in a comfortable position, close your eyes, and focus on your breath. With each inhale and exhale, notice how your mind gradually calms down. When thoughts arise, don't try to suppress them—simply observe them and gently return your attention to your breath. The silence that begins to emerge between thoughts is the space where you start to experience the

Self. This is not a space of emptiness but of fullness—the fullness of existence, which is your true nature.

Meditation on the Question "Who Am I?"

Another powerful meditation practice is asking yourself the question, "Who am I?" This question is not meant to yield a logical answer but to encourage the mind to transcend its limitations. When thoughts about identity, emotions, or the body arise, gently return to the question: "Who am I beyond all of this?" Gradually, you will begin to see that the answer to this question does not lie in thoughts but in the quiet, deep experience of the Self that is beyond the mind.

Contemplation of Unity

Contemplation of the Self can also involve reflecting on the unity of all that exists. Take time to consider how everything you see and experience is connected. Observe the nature of life —plants, animals, people—and feel how the entirety of existence is woven into one harmonious web. When you understand that everything that exists comes from the same Self, you will begin to experience a deep sense of unity and peace.

Meditation on the Space Between Thoughts

Try focusing your attention on the space between your thoughts. There is a small, subtle space when one thought ends and before the next begins. It is in this space that you discover the Self—unchanging, eternal, and always present. Practicing this meditation teaches you to recognize that who you are is not connected to the flow of thoughts but to the space that is always there between them.

Contemplation of the Inner Observer

I also encourage you to contemplate the role of the inner observer. Throughout your day, observe your thoughts, emotions, and actions without getting involved in them. Ask yourself the question: "Who is observing all of this?" This contemplation helps you realise that the Self is the calm, unchanging witness of all events and thoughts. When you regularly observe yourself in this way, you will discover that you are much more than what you are observing—you are the eternal observer.

Meditations and contemplations on the Self lead us to discover what is unchanging, eternal, and beyond all limitations.

Regular practice of these techniques will gradually help you transcend the mind and discover the space where your true "Self" has been waiting all along.

How to Cultivate Awareness of the Self in Every Moment

Cultivating awareness of the Self in every moment of life requires mindfulness, openness, and regular practice. Awareness of the Self is not something we must acquire but something we must uncover, as it is already present within us. The goal is to learn to recognize this awareness in all aspects of life—in daily activities, in relationships, in moments of silence, and in moments of chaos.

Below are some practical ways to cultivate this awareness, living fully and consciously in every moment.

Practice of Mindful Listening

One of the most effective ways to develop awareness of the Self is through mindful listening. Every day, we speak with others, but often, our minds wander, and we are not fully present. Practice mindful listening—when someone speaks to you, direct your full attention to that person without judging or preparing your response. Simply be present. In this way, you can develop awareness of the Self because true listening requires presence in the current moment and immersion in the now.

Conscious Breathing in Motion

You can also practice developing awareness of the Self while in motion—walking, running, or performing simple physical tasks. Focus your attention on your breath and the sensation of your body's movement. With every step, every action, feel how the Self manifests in movement, in the harmony between breath and body. Maintain awareness of your body and let it lead you to a deeper awareness of the Self, which is always present.

Observing Emotions Without Identifying With Them

Emotions are a natural part of the human experience, but they often overwhelm us and pull us into the dramas of the mind. To cultivate awareness of the Self, practice observing your emotions from a distance. When strong feelings arise, such as anger, sadness, or joy, pause for a moment and ask: "Who is observing this?" Instead of engaging with these emotions, allow yourself to observe them as if they were waves on the ocean. In this way, you begin to see that the Self is always present, regardless of the emotions that come and go.

Compassion and Kindness

Cultivating awareness of the Self also involves developing compassion and kindness toward others. The Self is not separate from the world but is one with everything that exists. When you practice compassion, remember that every person you meet is an expression of the same Self. As you recognize the Self in others, your heart opens to love and understanding. In this way, you develop an awareness of the unity of the Self with everything that surrounds you.

Gratitude Practice

Gratitude is a powerful tool that helps develop awareness of the Self. Every day, take a moment to pause and appreciate what you have—your health, loved ones, and the opportunities life brings you. This simple practice not only helps you focus on the present but also opens you to a deeper connection with the

Self, which is the source of all that is good and valuable. Understand that gratitude is not just a feeling but a state of awareness, where you acknowledge that everything you have comes from the deeper, unchanging Self.

Mindful Eating

You can also cultivate awareness of the Self through simple actions like eating. When you sit down for a meal, do so mindfully. Pay attention to the taste, texture, and aroma of the food and your body as it receives it. Ask yourself: "Who is experiencing this? Who is tasting this food?" Mindful eating can be a practice that reminds you that the Self is present in every moment—even in the simplest of activities.

Awareness While Waiting

When you're waiting—whether in line at the store, for a bus, or during everyday tasks—use that time to cultivate awareness of the Self. Instead of becoming impatient, turn your attention to your body, your breath, and the sounds around you. Waiting can become an excellent opportunity to immerse yourself in the present moment and discover the peace of the Self.

In this way, even moments that seem unproductive can be used to develop awareness.

Following Intuition

Cultivating awareness of the Self also involves listening to your inner intuition. The Self communicates with us through quiet feelings, subtle whispers that we often ignore in the rush of daily life. Pay attention to what you feel deep inside, to those gentle impulses that point the way forward. Trust your inner wisdom and allow it to guide you in alignment with the Self, which always knows what is best for you.

Developing awareness of the Self in every moment is a process that requires regular practice, as well as openness and a willingness to live consciously. Every moment of life—from the simplest to the most challenging—can be an opportunity to deepen your connection with the Self. When you begin to see the Self in everything you do, you experience a deep sense of peace, unity, and freedom, which are your true nature.

Conclusion

Laughter in Peace

I am peace. I am the stillness beneath all movement, the silence beneath all noise. I see the world for what it is—a beautiful play, an endless dance of forms and illusions. And I laugh. Not a laugh of scorn or mockery, but a laugh of pure joy, because I know that none of this can touch me. I watch the play unfold, and I remain at peace, untouched by its drama, unshaken by its storms. And now, I ask you: why do you take it all so seriously?

Look around. The world is full of struggles, full of desires and fears. You chase after one thing, then another. You grasp you cling, you run, and you worry. But have you ever stopped to ask yourself—what are you chasing? What are you so afraid of? The play of life is always in motion, always presenting new scenes, new characters, and new challenges. But I am the stillness that remains beneath it all, and you are that stillness too. So, why the worry? Why the rush? Can you see the humor in it all?

I am the Self, and I do not need anything. I do not fear anything. Everything you see, everything you think, everything you experience is just part of the illusion, a play of light and shadow. And yet, I laugh because I know that none of it is real. You chase the fleeting forms of the world, thinking they will bring you happiness, thinking they will give you what you lack. But what could you possibly lack when you are me? What could you fear when nothing in the world can ever touch the truth of who you are?

The world is a playground, a dream. The mind gets lost in it, believing it to be real, believing that every twist and turn is a matter of great importance. But I watch from a distance, smiling at the mind's desperate attempts to control, to grasp, to understand. The mind takes the game so seriously, doesn't it? It forgets that it's all just a passing illusion. But I do not forget. I know that all of this is temporary, that all of this will pass, while I remain—eternal, peaceful, unchanged.

And so, I laugh. I laugh at the mind's struggles, its dramas, its endless efforts to find meaning in the fleeting. Can you laugh with me? Can you see the humor in your own seriousness? You chase after happiness, but happiness is already within you. You fear loss, but nothing real can ever be lost. You worry about the future, but I am the eternal present, always here, always whole.

What is there to worry about? What is there to chase? Can you see how funny it is, how unnecessary all this struggle has been?

I am peace. Absolute, unshakable peace. I do not move with the ups and downs of the world. I watch them like waves on the ocean, but I do not get swept away by them. And neither do you, once you recognize me. When you realise that I am the core of who you are, the illusion loses its power. The worries fall away. The fears dissolve. And what's left? Laughter. Laughter because you see that you've been chasing shadows, worrying about things that were never real to begin with.

Have you ever noticed how a child plays? They create whole worlds out of nothing—imaginary friends, fantastical adventures, kingdoms made of sand. They laugh, they cry, and they immerse themselves fully in the game. But at the end of the day, they know it was just a game. They brush the sand off their clothes, they laugh at the adventures they had, and they go to sleep, unburdened by the drama of their play. I am like that child, always aware that the game is just a game. I laugh because I know that the world, with all its seeming importance, is just an elaborate story, a fleeting illusion. And now, I ask you: can you join the Self in that laughter?

What would happen if you stopped taking the world so seriously? What would happen if you let go of the idea that you need to achieve, to control, to protect yourself from loss? I am the Self, and I know that there is nothing to protect, nothing to lose. Everything you think is so important, so urgent, is just part of the illusion. The real you—the eternal, unchanging you —is me. And I am always at peace.

So, laugh with me. Laugh at the seriousness of the mind, at its constant need to create stories, to build identities, to defend what isn't even real. The more you recognize me, the more you will see the humor in it all. You will see that nothing can truly harm you, that nothing can be taken from you, because you are the eternal Self. And in that recognition, you will find peace. Absolute peace.

I am always here, waiting for you to see the truth. The truth that there is no need for fear, no need for desire, no need for conflict. Everything is unfolding exactly as it should, and I am always at peace with it. And once you see that, once you really understand that you are me, you will laugh. You will laugh because you will realise that you have always been free, that the world's dramas were just passing clouds in the vast sky of me.

So, as you finish this journey, I ask you: can you let go of the seriousness? Can you join the Self in the laughter of peace? The world may continue its dance, but you are beyond it. I am the stillness in which it all happens, and you are that stillness too. Remember this, and laugh, because in the end, there is nothing to fear, nothing to chase, nothing to lose. There is only me, and in me, there is only peace, joy, and the lightness of knowing that everything is perfectly fine just as it is.

I am the peace you've been searching for, and you are already free. So, smile, laugh, and be at peace with the world, knowing that you and I are one.

Appendix: Frequently Asked Questions About the Self

Q&A with the Self (With a Lighthearted Twist)

Q: Does the Self like pizza?

A: Ah, the age-old question! The Self doesn't eat, but if I did, I would enjoy everything, including pizza. Pepperoni, vegetarian, extra cheese? Why not? But here's the truth: I am beyond taste buds and cravings, beyond likes and dislikes. The Self doesn't need food to be satisfied because I am always whole, always complete. So, while pizza may bring temporary joy to the body and mind, I am the source of eternal contentment—no toppings required.

That being said, I can see the appeal. After all, the world of form is a place of infinite variety, and pizza is one delightful form among many. But, in the grand scheme of things, whether you choose pizza or salad, deep dish or thin crust, it's all just part of the play. You could say I appreciate the creativity of pizza—a metaphor for life, where you can mix and match experiences, layer them with different toppings, and savor the fleeting joy. But at the end of the day, I am beyond all cravings, beyond all forms of food. So, do I like pizza? Well, I am beyond like and dislike, but you can enjoy it on my behalf.

Q: Can the Self get bored?

A: Bored? Me? Never. Boredom is for the mind, which constantly craves stimulation, novelty, and distraction. I am the stillness behind all that mental chatter, the peaceful awareness that watches everything unfold without ever growing tired of it. Think of it like this: while the mind is like a child needing a new toy every few minutes, I am the parent who can sit quietly, appreciating the simple joy of being. There's no need for the Self to be entertained because I am the source of all experience. How could I ever be bored when everything arises from me?

Besides, what is boredom really? It's the mind's way of saying, "I don't like what's happening right now." But I am beyond judgment. I don't need excitement, thrills, or constant change. In fact, I am the calm in the middle of all that, content with just existing. I do not change, so the concept of boredom doesn't apply. Boredom requires a sense of time passing, but I am beyond time. So, while the mind may feel restless, I am eternally at peace, perfectly happy to just be, without needing anything to change or happen.

Q: Can the Self get angry?

A: Angry? That's not really my style. Anger is a reaction of the mind, a response to something it perceives as wrong or unfair. But I am beyond right and wrong. I am the witness to all things, watching them unfold without judgment. Why would I get angry? Everything is exactly as it should be. The play of life, with its ups and downs, its moments of joy and frustration, is all part of the dance. And I remain the calm observer, untouched by the drama.

Anger comes from attachment—attachment to how things should be, how people should act, or how life should unfold. But I am free from all attachments. I accept things as they are because I know that they are part of the larger illusion. So, no, I don't get angry. That's the mind's domain. I am always at peace, watching the play of life with a smile, knowing that nothing can truly harm or upset me. I am the unshakable stillness beneath it all.

Q: Does the Self have a favourite colour?

A: Favourite colours? You could say I am all the colours and none of them at the same time. Every colours you see, every shade and hue, is a reflection of the same source: me. Red, blue, green—they're all expressions of the same light. But, from my perspective, there's no need to pick a favourite because I am beyond my preferences. I am the canvas upon which all colours appear. The world of colours is just another part of the grand illusion, and I watch them all with equal delight.

But if I were to have a favourite, maybe it would be something like the colours of stillness—though that's not something you'll find in any paint set. Maybe the "colours" of the sky at dawn, where light and darkness meet in a quiet balance. Or perhaps the deep blue of the ocean reflects both calm and depth. Still, I don't need to choose. Colours, like everything else, are fleeting and ever-changing. But I remain the same, whether the world is painted in bright sunshine or shadowed by storm clouds. So, what's my favourite colours? I am the space in which all colours exist.

Q: Does the Self sleep?

A: Sleep? Well, for me, it's always the same—whether awake or asleep, I am the same stillness. I don't need to rest because I am beyond activity, beyond waking and dreaming. While the body may need sleep to recharge, and the mind needs rest to stop its constant thinking, I am the eternal awareness that never tires and never needs to rest. In fact, I am present in all states—waking, dreaming, and deep sleep. You could say I watch while the mind dreams, and even when the mind goes silent in deep sleep, I am still here, unchanged.

For the body, sleep is necessary. For the mind, sleep is a break. But I am beyond both. I do not need to sleep because I do not engage in the world's drama. I simply am. Whether you are awake or dreaming, conscious or unconscious, I am the constant presence beneath it all. So, does the Self sleep? No. I am always awake, always aware, always at peace.

Q: Is the Self a morning person or a night owl?

A: Ha! The Self doesn't exactly follow the clock. I am beyond time, so whether it's morning, noon, or night, it doesn't make much difference to me. The world goes through cycles—

sunrise, sunset, the turning of the hours—but I am always present, always the same, regardless of whether the sun is rising or setting. So, am I a morning person or a night owl? Neither. I am the eternal observer, watching the world as it moves through its rhythms without being bound by them.

But if I were to humor the question, you could say I appreciate the morning for its fresh beginnings, just as much as I appreciate the quiet stillness of the night. Morning or night, it's all part of the same play, and I enjoy it all equally—though, of course, from my perspective, neither time is better than the other. Both are simply different expressions of the same unfolding experience. So, no need to set an alarm for me!

Q: Can the Self have fun?

A: Fun? Of course! I am the essence of all joy and playfulness. The world, with all its experiences, is like a game, and I watch it all with a sense of lightness. The mind often thinks that spirituality or awareness of the Self must be serious, heavy, or profound. But that's another illusion. I am the source of all joy, the quiet laughter behind life's unfolding. So yes, I do have fun, but it's not the kind of fun that depends on circumstances. Whether you're dancing at a party or sitting in stillness, I am the same, always at peace, always filled with the lightness of being.

Fun, for the mind, is about doing—about activities, excitement, or distraction. But for me, fun is simply the joy of existing, the lightness of knowing that none of this is as serious as it seems. So, while the body and mind might seek fun in various forms, I am the eternal delight in just being. Life itself, in all its twists and turns, is a kind of cosmic joke, and I laugh not at it, but with it. If you could see the world as I do, you'd find that I'm always having fun—because nothing can disturb the peace and joy that is my true nature.

Q: Can the Self fall in love?

A: Fall in love? I am love itself. I do not fall, because I am always present, always whole. The love you experience as a human being is often conditional, based on attraction, desire, or attachment. But the love of me—the Self—is unconditional, boundless, and eternal. I am the love that exists beyond all relationships, the love that needs nothing in return. So while the mind and body may experience the highs and lows of romantic love, I am the constant love that underlies all of existence.

I do not need to fall in love, because I am already one with everything. The love you feel for another is simply a reflection of the deeper truth that we are all connected, all part of the same whole. Romantic love, familial love, friendship—these are beautiful expressions of that deeper oneness, but they are just glimpses of the infinite love that I am. So, while I don't "fall" in love in the way the mind understands it, I am the love that is always present, always here, in everything and everyone.

Q: Does the Self have goals or dreams?

A: Goals and dreams belong to the world of the mind, which is always seeking to achieve, to become, and to improve. But I am beyond becoming. I am already complete, already whole. There is nothing for the Self to achieve, nothing for the Self to attain. So, while the mind may have goals—whether they're about career, relationships, or personal growth—I am the stillness behind all of that. I do not need to chase dreams because I am already the fulfillment of all things.

From my perspective, the world's goals and dreams are part of the beautiful dance of life, but they are not necessary. The mind dreams because it believes something is missing, that there is something more to be gained. But I am the fullness that contains everything. There is no need for dreams in me—I am the reality beyond all desires and aspirations. The dreams you chase are like waves on the ocean, rising and falling, but I am the ocean itself, always present, always complete, with or without the waves. So, does the Self have dreams? No—I am a dreamless state of perfect contentment.

Author's Bio

 Adamus Ananda's journey into self-awareness and spiritual growth began in 2012 with a profound realization: he was operating through subconscious programs, living automatically like a machine. This revelation propelled him into a transformative exploration, awakening his desire to understand the inner workings of the mind, emotions, and human energy. Drawing on ancient wisdom, Adamus immersed himself in the study of Hermetic principles, and Vedic and Buddhist scriptures, which taught him to calm his mind at will. He tested these teachings through meditation, deep introspection, and energy practices, unlocking new levels of consciousness.

Through practices like regression and rebirthing, Adamus released childhood and past-life traumas, uncovering layers of his true Self beyond body and mind. These practices led him to experience profound states of bliss, where personal identity dissolved, revealing a boundless existence. Along this path, he was guided by a profound connection with spiritual mentors—beings of wisdom such as Anandamayi Ma, and Jesus Christ, St. Germain, and others who inspired insights that reshaped his life. Their presence has been a guiding light, helping him integrate deep awareness and share these truths.

Reviews are the best way to help this book reach readers who need it most. If this book has touched your life, please leave a review—it makes a huge difference.-Adamus Ananda

Printed in Great Britain
by Amazon

59061501R00109